STEELFLOWER
AT SEA

STEELFLOWER
AT SEA

LILITH
SAINTCROW

DEDICATION

To Skyla, who believes.

BLESSING, CURSE

THE FAT-SAILED HIGH-PROWED *TARYAM'AJAK* of Antai bit salt swells, singing of rigging and canvas strained by pressure, bound for home across the wide blue desert of the Lan'ai. I braced myself against the railing, ocean's song stripping my braids back with steady chill fingers. Night on the back of the restless sea-mare folded around me, clouds scudding scarves for the Moon's silver face and stars filling a sky made limitless by the heaving backs of waves underneath. Even on the Danhai plains, that great grass sea, the sky can drive a Shainakh mad. I had seen more than a few cases of such sickness—*kair'la*.

The *Taryam* dipped his prow and rose, cutting cleanly through a wave. The Antai call their ships *he*, since they cleave the Lan'ai, that great blue-breasted goddess. Anything at the mercy of such a divine female must, to them, necessarily be a man.

Wave-song, the salt-breath, and the creak of rigging and timber all have a power to calm. Normally I would be in a hammock belowdecks, dreaming of flight as I often did while a-ship. I wanted nothing more than to lose myself in sleep's foreign country—my eyes were grainy, my shoulders tight as rigging cables, my *dotani* heavy against my back.

After a battle, sellsword and enlisted soldier alike crave unconsciousness. The Shainakh call that weariness and its product *hath'ar lak*.

It is also the word for a death of sleepy old age, in a bed, surrounded by loved ones.

Every time I closed my eyes, I heard a throat-scouring scream across a dust-choked plain.

"You're my luck! You can't *leave! The gods told me!* My luck will turn against me! Kaia!*" Rikyat's voice, unfurling across the battlefield. The moans of the dying, and the smell of battle—*

I wrapped my fingers as far as they would reach around the top of the deckrail, whitened knuckles standing out, thread-thin knife scars even paler. My shoulder twinged briefly—the left, where a shallow, newly healed slice reminded me of how close I'd come to being used.

Would it have been so gods-be-damned difficult for a man to *ask*? There was precious little I would not have done for Ammerdahl Rikyat, had he simply told me what he planned and what was necessary.

"You should be sleeping." Darik stood beside me, not leaning against the railing, blue-black hair pushed back from his coppery forehead by the wind's ungentle fingers, the twin hilts of *dotanii* rising over his shoulders. Even on a merchant ship, travel-stained and weary, he looked every fingerwidth the prince. Heir to the Dragon Throne of G'mai, nephew of the queen, warlord and strategist... and my *s'tarei*. Me, the only flawed G'mai, the only woman of my kind to travel alone.

Not alone, now. If it was blessing or curse, I could not yet tell. Neither, I suspected, could he.

I shrugged, unclenching my fingers briefly from salt-scoured wood to tuck a stray braid back into its proper place. I would have to thread more twine through the hair-ropes to keep the mass secured. "So should you," I pointed out, and heard the sharpness. Ever a blade drawn, the edges behind the words just as likely to flay as to lance a boil.

An edge can heal, the Clau say, and healers carry knives. I wondered if a word could do the same. It never seems to.

The stinging wind veered a point or two, spray fanning high as the prow dipped afresh, and I scanned the moonlit surface as if it were the rolling grass of the Plains, and the Danhai tribesmen swimming in its depths, like the sawtooth highfins the Hain make their curative soup from. Rising to strike the unwary, the only warning a curious quiet before the bolts begin to fly or the knifeblade plunges into a sleeping sentry's throat.

A sellsword learns to sense the moment before violence strikes. At least, if she means to survive.

Slowly, cautiously, Darik slid his right arm around me, his left flattening along my ribs over the shadow of the last strike of our duel in Vulfentown—the duel that had brought me to twinsickness, nearly killing both of us. "All is well, K'li." A murmur of G'mai poured into the hollow of my ear, sharp consonants and liquid vowels blurring together.

The shortening of my given name as well as the inflection, unbearably intimate, might have spilled a shiver down my back. I denied it. For well over ten winters my birth-tongue had not crossed my lips, until *he* appeared. Yet it had begun to seem almost natural to use its rhythm again. "I wish I could be so certain."

"*I* know. Is that not enough?" He rested his chin atop my head. I am slightly taller than the average G'mai female, broader at shoulder and hip from years of practice and sellswording, any slimness is deceptive. Darik, however, is slightly larger than most G'mai males, which meant he was several weights heavier and a head-

and-a-half taller than even an ill-tempered marshcat of a sellsword.

It made him a comforting wall, his boots braced against the deck, moving with me as the ship rolled across the waves. His left hand tensed slightly. He was in the habit lately of touching the scar, where his *dotanii* had flicked down my ribs and bit.

Each time he did so, I allowed it for a little longer, and a little longer still.

His warmth made rest seem a possibility. The rest of them were bedded down safely enough—Janaire and Atyarik sharing a hammock, Redfist the giant red barbarian bedded in a pile of blankets between two crates carrying goods I didn't ask the provenance of, Diyan the erstwhile Vulfentown wharf-rat curled against Redfist's side. I did not blame him, for the barbarian was heat aplenty, even though he smelled somewhat ripe. And, to round out the entire sorry troupe, Gavrin the Pesh minstrel lay wrapped in blankets an arm's length from Redfist. He dozed, I supposed, between fits of shipsick heaving.

He would no doubt write a grand clanging epic about said sickness and subject us to it as soon as we reached Antai.

I had not slept for three days. And before, on the long ride back to Vulfentown, I had barely rested at all. I had convinced Janaire to keep giving me the *taih'adai*— the starmetal spheres that would give me the knowledge of how to use Power, the birthright of all G'mai women.

I had only three of the last set of seven *taih'adai* to endure before I could...what?

It is not battle that unnerves a sellsword most. Tis the *waiting*. Uncertainty can breed its own madness. I could not think of a word in Shainakh that fit, nor in the mouth-of-mush that is Hain, or the sibilants of Pesh. There wasn't even a satisfactory word in G'mai for it.

"Come below, K'li." Softly, conciliatory, as if he feared I would turn on him. "There is no danger here. When will we reach port?"

I leaned back, into his chest. Two days from Vulfentown and about to hit the Shelt, shallows falling away beneath the *Taryam'ajak*'s keel. The great swells would start soon, the ship running with the wind, and Gavrin would be even sicker, unless he adjusted.

Sometimes, they did. The first time I had voyaged across the Lan'ai, my own stomach had hated the liquid heaving of unland. "Sixteen days, most likely twenty. The wind and the wave have the say of it, not us." The proverb sounded different in G'mai. In the tradetongue it is a marvel of succinct sound, two Shainakh nouns and a Pesh loan-verb shortened into the imperative, and a third term nobody could tell the provenance of. In G'mai, it could be phrased four or five ways, each with a different twist, but I was weary and chose the least poetic of them all.

With Darik behind me, the sea's breath did not seem so chill. Even a sellsword thief worth much red Shainakh gold reaches the limits of endurance, sooner or later. I had not truly rested since Hain, when I'd picked a barbarian's pocket and found myself pursued.

"Come." His inflection was gentle, and made the word almost a question instead of a command.

I let him work my fingers free of the rail, his hands callused as mine from swordplay. I let him lead me belowdeck, into our rented corner of the hold. Kesamine at the Swallows Moon Inn had found us passage to Antai on a merchant ship with little fuss. The captain was a Drava's-kin, and so beholden to Kesa, and the enticement of having four G'mai and a barbarian with an axe made up for the extra useless mouths—a wharf-rat and a minstrel who had already proved to be shipsick.

The extra blades I provided would be welcome if unluck in the form of pirates struck.

As for the rest, we'd paid in good red gold. Many thanks to Ammerdahl Rikyat, there was enough and to spare.

My luck will turn against me!

One barred chest wedged against Redfist's back contained two hundred forty-eight Shainakh red Rams now, a merchant lord's ransom. I had wanted to dump it in the Shainakh army camp, but Janaire and Atyarik overruled me. By the time we had bedded down that night on the coastal plain, it had been too late to argue.

Better to use the gold than waste it, Janaire said firmly.

I would lose my reputation as a thief if I threw away good red gold for a silly little point of honor, too. Not to mention winter looming, and this small collection of outcasts looking to me for food and shelter.

Perhaps it was my payment for the tangle I found myself in. Solid land turning to sea underfoot, a *s'tarei* of my own and the birthright of my kind, the one thing I had always lacked, offered to me with open palms. I could not help but peer at the giver and wait for the luck to be snatched away.

Wandering the world had taught me very little is given freely, and that which is often has a sting in the tail.

My own rented hammock swung gently with the motion of the ship, but I dropped my sword-harness to one side and collapsed atop Darik's sleeping-roll. I fussed with the blankets while Darik unbuckled his own sword-harness and laid it down with finicky precision, lowered himself gingerly beside me.

As long as I had been awake, he had been with me, uncomplaining.

I was too exhausted to pretend, anymore. I waited until he had settled himself; I rolled close to his side, carrying my share of blankets along too. The wooden floor was hard and swaying, but at least there were no stones beneath the sleeping-roll, and with his heat beside me I would not wake in the late watches shivering.

We both kept our boots on. You do not sleep without your footgear unless you are *certain*.

I much doubted I would ever be certain of anything, ever again.

It took rearranging, but we finally settled, my head on his shoulder, my eyes closed, my arm thrown loosely across his chest, a knifehilt supporting my elbow. Yet another measure of our accord, that we would both sleep with blades to hand.

It is never wise to do otherwise on a ship, even one you may trust the captain of. I learned as much my first stomach-churning time across the Lan'ai, and took the lesson to heart. I still had the scar up my ribs, a skittering knifeblade in the dark and the fear, Mother Moon, the *fear*.

"There," D'ri whispered, quietly enough I almost missed the word under the sounds of wood creaking and the gurgle against the ship's thin wooden skin. "We are all safe, for the time being."

I nodded, my braids digging into his shoulder. If it was uncomfortable, he made no sign, and I did not feel it. "Thank the Moon," I murmured, in sleepy G'mai. "My luck is due to be better soon."

That earned a small laugh, rumbling against my ear. "Rest, Kaia." His hand came up. I think he meant to stroke my hair, but instead his fingertips found my cheek, and he stopped, calluses barely touching. "Your *s'tarei* will stand watch."

"You should..." I could not take him to task as thoroughly as he deserved. I fell into blackness without even a grateful sigh.

Does Not Bear Mentioning

"HOLD IT *SO*." I REACHED over Diyan's shoulder to correct his grip on the knifehilt. "As if you have a hand clasped in yours. Not so tight; it will be torn away. There. Now, again."

The afternoon sun glittered; after a slackening at nooning, a freshening wind filled the canvas. The skinny boy pawed dark hair out of his eyes and tried again, an upward slash. "Good." I moved behind him, pushing him forward. "Never forget your feet. Half a knife-fight is won below the knees."

"'Ware your side, young one," pale Rainak Redfist said gruffly, from his easy crouch in the lee of a coiled rope. Sea travel agreed with him. He looked actually *happy*, his red beard curling with the spray and his bulk more graceful than many a land-dweller could claim to be. It brought out the ruddiness in his floury cheeks as well, and if his leather jerkin was often sodden, he bore it with a smile.

Gavrin the Pesh minstrel, his dirty-straw hair slicked with sweat, heaved desperately over the side. Janaire, her soft Gavridar face expressionless, held her hand over his shoulder. Power rang under her palm, sinking into the young man's shaking body. "Gods," he groaned, and added something highly impolite in his native tongue.

Pesh are filthy-mouthed, and former slaves doubly so. Even the sailors were in awe of the minstrel's command of obscenities in both his own Pesh *and* tradespeak. Perhaps it was a function of his craft.

Lean long-faced Atyarik sat cross-legged and iron-spined on the deck next to the copper-furred barbarian, watching me teach the boy. He occasionally glanced at Janaire, but she had the minstrel well in hand. The Northern giant and the Tyaanismir *s'tarei* understood each other in the way of old sellswords, and their ease with each other relieved me of any responsibility to speak overmuch to either of them.

Still, it irked me, a little. Since I'd picked Redfist's pocket that night in Hain, I hadn't had a moment's comfortable solitude, but...well, I almost missed the forest and only a giant Northerner causing me problems, instead of a group of lagging sheep to feed, clothe, and care for. That the sheep preferred their own society to mine was to be expected, but still.

The wind bore no shrieking, yet beaten-iron clouds raced on either side. The crew were all nervous, smelling change. If the clouds closed on us, most of my charges would be belowdecks while a storm tossed the ship about. "Good," I told the boy, and he preened. Salt air, free movement, and a larger supply of food had done wonders for his frame. He had grown like a mirinweed these past few weeks, though how much of that was his laying aside the wharf-rat habit of slouching in shadows I could not guess. He also hid small bits of travel-bread, or salted meat, in his pockets until they moldered.

Hunger does strange things, especially to the young. I pretended not to notice, and he sometimes, shamefaced, crept to the railing to drop the crumbling bits into the

Lan'ai's embrace. "Now, hold like *so*, step with your foot *thus*, and move *here*. Good. Again."

He obeyed with good grace, but as soon as he started, a shout rose from portside. I straightened swiftly, almost knocking the boy over, set him on his feet with absent care. Even growing, he was still a slight lad.

Darik, his hands occupied with a whetstone and a slightly-curved smallknife, glanced at me.

"Keep going," I told the boy. "D'ri, drill him?"

He nodded, pushing straight black hair from his severely beautiful Dragaemir features. I would find a means of trimming his mane soon as we approached land. An *adai*'s duty, one I had neglected as I had so many others. There was much to berate myself for, should I ever decide to start doing so in earnest.

I negotiated the slippery wood to the captain's deck, waited for Hrufel's nod of acknowledgement, and climbed up the three last stairs to his unchallenged fiefdom. "Ai," he growled at his *adjii*, and added something I might have blushed to repeat, lowering a farlooker of wood, brass, and ground glass. I followed his line, almost turning my back to him.

But not quite.

G'mai have excellent vision. Three specks, moving fast with the wind, bearing down on us. My heart sank. "That does not seem a merchant convoy."

Hrufel grunted and handed me the farlooker, its leather case dangling from a strap at his belt. I peered through, though I already suspected what I would find.

Three ships, bearing black and red pennons, one suspiciously low in the water.

Well. "Mother's *tits*." I didn't even have the heart to curse properly.

"May decide we're slim pickins," the Shainakh adjii, his rat-nested hair hung with charms against ill-luck, offered. He did not sound exceedingly hopeful.

"And Pesh priglets may well fly out me arse," Hrufel snorted, a gleam behind his lips the gold tooth he was always licking. "Yer crew ready fer mixin, Iron Flower?" His heavy-accented tradetongue butchered the use-name, but at least he didn't use the phrase that rhymed with "*metal cunt*" in sailor's argot.

"Oh, of course." I grinned broadly, showing all my teeth, none of them gold-capped but fine enough. "You have three tested blades and one G'mai witch, and a barbarian giant to boot. We may well convince them there's nothing to be gained for the price they'd pay in blood."

"Nae chance yon elvish witch can rise a storm and founder 'em?" The adjii picked at the corner of his lip with blunt fingertips.

A spark of irritation struck itself below my breastbone, died for lack of air. Mother Moon, I *hated* that word. "Any storm raised might founder the *Taryam* as well. Surely you're not eager for that."

Hrufel hissed for him to be quiet. "Well, if there's witchery about, what *can* ye do?"

"Give me a moment." I almost saluted in the manner of the Shainakh irregulars, caught myself, and set off for the other side of the ship.

Darik read trouble in my expression and halted; the boy almost dropped his blade. I beckoned Janaire, whose pretty face drained of color, as if she suspected trouble. "*Yada'Adais.* I request your assistance." My inflection was honorific, extremely so. Teachers are held in high regard among the people of G'maihallan, and none more so than those who could school *adai* in the ways of Power. It takes patience, fearlessness, and firmness in almost equal measure, and heavy helpings of each.

Janaire exchanged a glance with her *s'tarei,* who unfolded from Redfist's lee and was at her side in two swift strides. He said something too low for me to hear, and I glanced at Darik, whose eyebrows rose a fraction. *I do not know, K'li.* His tone was intimate, the *taran'adai* a warmth in my head, and I no longer shuddered to hear the voice-within. *Trouble?*

It was not often he spoke-within to me. *Too soon to tell,* I replied, soundlessly. Some *adai* may speak-within to beast and bird, others to other G'mai, and some very few to those not of the Moon's children. All, however, may speak with their *s'tarei* or *adai*; it is one of the first gifts of the twinning.

Shall I need my dotanii? As if the twin blades were not riding his shoulders, as always. Perhaps sea-travel did him well, too, for the tone held a distinct note of levity, and another of...the only word I could find was *joy*.

Of course. Tis your duty to watch my back, is it not? "Janaire?" I didn't move. She looked too pale, even for her.

"Nothing," she said. "Of course. Tis merely a shock, to be addressed as a Teacher."

I swallowed bitter impatience. Nothing moves quickly on the Lan'ai's back; they would not catch us for some hours yet. The minstrel groaned, hanging onto a barrel, and I found Diyan next to me, pressing against my hip as if he sought comfort. "Redfist?"

"Aye, lass?" The barbarian rose. "Methinks there's some bandits bearing down on us."

"Could be. Can you take Gavrin and Diyan belowdecks?"

He nodded. "If there is fightin', I'll nae be hiding below like a rat."

"I didn't ask you to." Still, the echo of D'ri's good mood lingered; the corners of my mouth had both tilted up. "You will see plenty of trouble above, should it find us, I simply wish our young ones out of the way. If you would follow me, *Yada'Adais*."

I turned on my heel, Darik falling into step behind me. "Negotiations, or a battle?"

Was this what other *adai* felt, when their twin was close and danger threatened? "Not much hope of the first." And now I had not only my own skin to look after, but theirs as well.

And his.

His reply was a wash of feeling too complex for words. The accord between *s'tarei and adai* was growing stronger between us, the *taran'adai* more pronounced. If it continued, how much of that solitude I told myself I needed in order to breathe properly would remain?

One disaster at a time, Kaia. I shook away distractions and set my jaw, waiting until Hrufel gestured us onto the captain's deck again. "Gavridar Taryana Janaire, the captain respectfully wonders if you might be able to solve a problem for us."

"I am glad to assist however I may." Very formally, her tradetongue bearing a strong sharp accent of G'mai, handling especially the Pesh loan-words gingerly, as if they might sting. She folded her hands before her, the oversleeves falling in a graceful line. The very picture of a proper *adai*, from the sharp tips of her ears to her low-dressed braids—much shorter than mine—and her supple, well-made G'mai traveling-boots.

Hrufel lowered the farseer. The color had gone out of his cheeks, leaving him the uneasy shade of cheese some Pesh-mixed Shainakh sometimes get. "Fuck a dog's mother. Red flag, two slash. It's Scoryin."

Now *that* was interesting. A long way away, under the bruise-darkening clouds, a single glitter of lightning flashed. "I thought he would be hunting around Clau this time of year." The habits of corsairs are changeable, though. On the Shelt, this late in the season, the risk of foundering your own small timber shelter was high enough to dissuade all but the stupid or desperate. Scoryin was not overly stupid, but a bad year could have made him perverse.

"Either him or one bearin' his flag." Hrufel eyed me, both of us moving in the same moment as the ship hit a wave. "It's said he fancies you, Iron Flower. Either tha' or he wants y'dead." He capped the farseer with a deft habitual motion.

Rumor and ballad, those twin wingwyrms. "I accidentally sprang him from a gaol in Antai once, but I doubt that will earn us a reprieve." My habit of not killing fellow prisoners outright during such exploits might need reconsidering. "Janaire, is there aught you may do to slow those ships?"

She barely considered the notion before shaking her head, her braids swinging. "Weatherworking is difficult enough. Perhaps a simple weaving of air and sea. Perhaps you could..."

Oh, no you don't. "My training is unfinished. This is the Shelt." *And our first day at sea I almost set fire to the mainsail.* She had agreed, after that, it would be best to wait for landfall for me resume said lessons, whether with her or with the starmetal spheres. Unused Power had swollen behind a wall of silence, the killing quiet that had descended upon me after the shock of my mother's death, and safely draining such a lump was best attempted somewhere...else. On land.

With none I might wound in the vicinity.

Janaire considered the situation afresh, her top lip caught briefly in her small, perfect teeth as her dark gaze turned inward. The riverfolk of my home often look merry even while thoughtful, and she was no exception. "Practically speaking, if you failed, there would still be a fully trained *adai* aboard to deal with attackers."

A pragmatic point, and yet. "I'm worth more with a blade." I ran a thumb over a scar on my opposite knuckles, the broken nail scraping slightly.

"How much room, you reckon?" Hrufel licked his gold tooth, a quick flicker of pink. Freetowners do not generally have much in the way of beard, unless some Pesh creeps into their bloodline, but his cheeks were fast becoming forested.

His *adjii* scowled. "Fast little bitches." He glanced at the sky, and again at the waves. "With th' wind, as we are...Two hours."

Hrufel scratched at his pitted cheek. "Fuck a dog's mother," he repeated, morosely. "Ready the boys for action and lay out the cloth."

"*All ri' ye swine!*" the *adjii* bellowed, shoving past me. "*Lay out sheet, ho there!*" He began to swear in earnest, and the deck woke in a scurrying.

Hrufel stumped away to take the huge ebonwood wheel from the wrightson, who hopped off nimbly to other duties. The black-bearded captain did not glance our way again. At least he considered me capable enough to direct my own. Reputation was *occasionally* useful.

"Well, *adai'sa?*" I still used the honorific inflection, but the words took an edge between my mouth and the air, despite my intentions.

Her cheeks were white, bloodless, but it simply made her look ethereal. Beauty is bred into the Moon's children, and the lowlanders are not carved from stone as the mountainfolk. Their loveliness lies in a softness, and some called the lowlander features *aglai'sh*, the word for a child's roundness.

She shook her head. *Her* braids never came loose. "I can try."

"Wonderful." I turned slightly, stared past her at the black specks bearing down on us. "My thanks, *Yada'Adais.*"

Her chin came up, her braids shifting in the breeze. Atyarik, glowering, caught Darik's gaze and held his tongue. He contented himself with moving closer to Janaire, who brushed past me with a graceful flutter of skirts.

21

She was a flawless example of a G'mai *adai*, and I was merely a sellsword, battered by blade and bruise.

You do not care, Kaia. You have told yourself as much for weeks, now. "Ready yourself for battle then," I called after her. "And for the sake of every god that ever was, do *not* let yourself be captured. What they do to foreign witches does not bear mentioning."

THE RULE OF
SHIPBOARD

RUDDY SUNSET, BLOOD UPON THE sea. Sting of smoke in the throat, a heaving slipperiness underneath, wooden planks suddenly the twitching backskin of a live creature, and shouting, struggling, bleeding men mere fleas upon it. Two lean wolf-hungry corsairs with grapples, plus the low-lying *brota* for loading with spoil, closed for what they no doubt hoped was the kill. Arrows whistling, Hrufel screaming a sailor's warcry, Rainak Redfist charging across the deck with his dripping axe raised—a fearsome sight indeed.

One of the grapples held, its line curving with just a bit of slack since the *brota* had blundered against the leeward side of the *Taryam*, a fan of blood flicked from my *dotani* as I met a climbing pirate—a black-tooth parchment-haired Clau, burned red and scoured until he held no resemblance to Kesa of the Swallow's Moon. Instead, he was a tar-daubed bag of bloodlust and ragged salt-crusted cloth, and his throat opened under my blade with little ado.

Then I was past, as Darik shouted something behind me. Bare feet would have been better for what I threw myself upon—the stretching line between ships, suddenly thread-thin as I flashed along it. The faster you go, the easier to keep upright, and there was *just* enough slack for it to accept my weight. The battle-madness was upon me, and I did not think of falling.

Kaia! Darik, inside my head, but I had no time to reassure him or anyone else. I landed with a jolt on the *brota*'s low deck, ducking under a stanchion-wielding bare-chested Hain's blow, my balance caught in that first crucial second. I took the only avenue of escape possible, tucking and *rolling*, my shredded shirtsleeve flapping—one of the boarding party had caught me with a knife, and the blood smoking down my arm was a spur. My *dotani* sang, cleaving air and meeting a short broad shipblade wielded by another Clau, this one's hair bleached to near-white. My foot flicked out, and my boots were useful again, one sinking into his belly, and I fish-jumped sideways with a wrenching effort. The one behind me wasn't going to be off-balance for long—

Splack. A black-fletched arrow bloomed in the Clau's eye, and I rolled further aside as the Hain lunged for me, bringing the stanchion down. Above, balanced on the *Taryam*'s railing, Darik nocked and let another arrow loose.

Get down! I wanted to scream as he rode the heaving with natural grace. *Protect yourself!*

The second arrow buried itself in the stanchion-wielder's back, and he howled, an animal sound lost in the chaos. Janaire was on the captain's deck, using Power to staunch the fires; I *felt* her like a thunderstorm against my eardrums. A distraction I could not afford, it slowed me.

Sideways, again, my next kick crunching against an ankle; its owner, a lean Pesh sellsword with a hooked blade and a length of rope in her clenched left fist, fell sideways and temporarily gave me a breathing space. I scrambled to my feet, and my objective—the half-covered shed in the *brota*'s midship—yawned. The *Taryam* heeled, and the line I'd danced down sang a high creaking note of strain.

Three left, including the Pesh sellsword. She was no doubt quick and brutal, if she'd survived childhood *and* signing on with pirates.

A thumping heartbeat reverberated along the deck. It was the drum in the small shed I aimed for, stroked by a lean one-eyed motherless scum with a seamed, half-bald head and rat bones tied in his dark topknot, clicking and clacking.

A windwitch. Worth his weight in gold, and probably chained to that drum. It was how even a *brota* could have caught up with the *Taryam* in the open sea—stroking that stretched skin, probably with a mouthful of *vavir*-weed, shaping the waves, the poor soul inside that noisome cave probably didn't even know where on the face of the world he was heave-drawn upon. Probably a gifted sailor who trusted the wrong shipmate and was taken, forced to the *vavir* and chained to a drum.

No wonder Scoryin's ships had been out this late upon the Shelt. Hrufel's craft, however, had turned out to have spines, and stuck in the attackers' throats.

The Pesh sellsword gained her feet with a lurching lunge, and I faded aside, shuffling, my free hand suddenly full of knifehilt. My largest knife, reversed along my forearm, because the other two were a pair of Shainakh, their black hair back with hanks of red thread. Their eyes were blank, the glow of sunset painting the deck with even more crimson and turning them to ochre-dipped statues.

A thump behind me. Another arrow flickered past, burying itself in a Shainakh's chest. The sailor's mouth dropped open, his proud, once-broken nose rising, and for a breathless moment he looked very much like Ammerdahl Rikyat. The second one lunged for me, and I caught a gleam at the very edge of the narrowing tunnel of battle-vision.

Hookblade whistling down—a hopefully broken ankle would not be enough to dissuade that Pesh sellsword—and I hopped aside, my *dotani* striking with a clash, just enough force to batter the hook aside. I crashed into her, my largest knife sinking in, muscle suction against the blade as I twisted, and now I had only the second Shainakh to deal with if I could simply *move* quickly enough.

The Pesh snarled in my face, exhaling a strange spiciness—her teeth were fine, toothpowder could be had in any port. She was young, too—the salt-crust and filth were rubbed into her skin to deter her shipmates from recreational rape. I wrenched the knife free, battlefield stink filling thick and rank in my nose, and snapped her knee with another kick. Her body fell away, my *dotani* flashing to open her throat on the way down as well, because that is the rule of shipboard battles.

It pays to be certain.

I whirled, *dotani* flashing up—

—and Darik's met it, with a slitherclash. He ran into me, driving me onto the sodden deck as something deadly whistled overhead. My head bounced, the titanic stink all over me, and he rolled aside, flowing into a crouch. The last Shainakh lay bleeding and gutsplit, moan-coughing blood as he stared at the spurting stump of his right arm.

What in the name of—

Another low sharp whistling sound, and a lance of pain rammed through my skull. My head snapped aside, blood flying from my nose, and I tumbled across dead and dying human tangles.

Darik launched himself into the midship shed, and I understood—the windwitch, striking with unphysical force. I thrashed, gaining my knees with more luck than skill, and the creaking line between the *brota* and the *Taryam* was not going to hold much longer, especially with the wind veering confusedly. More screams, and a roll of thunder from the north—had the windwitch staved off the storm until now, or were the twin arms of black cloud a result of witch-whispers?

The Lan'ai does not look upon such meddling kindly. The *Taryam* heeled afresh as the wind veered, breaking away from the windwitch's meddling.

Silence. Tiny droplets of crystalline salt-spray hung in midair, blood droplets too. The deck under me creaked and rose a few fingerwidths; I realized the remaining line to the merchant ship was pulling the flatter, lower craft up, and furthermore, the thrum-hop of the drum inside the cave had stopped.

I strained against the weight of that quiet, broke free with a crunch that tossed me across the suddenly slanting deck. A crimson flower bloomed as the sun slid fully below the horizon; the line to the *Taryam* broke and smoke gouted upward.

The brota slapped back onto the Lan'ai's surface, its hull cracking with a terrific noise. A tall staggering shadow was Darik, hauling a limp, dripping body from the cave.

Smoke. Where from?

Flaming wreckage fell like star-seeds, those molten pieces of heaven the *taih'adai* were made from. The smaller high-prowed corsair had swung around us, and it was burning merrily. Sailors screamed as they plunged from its deck, and I reached Darik just as the Lan'ai, tiring of our games, cracked the brota in half and sought to swallow us whole.

MORE IN COMMON

HE HEAVED, A GREAT GUSH of seawater foaming from mouth and nose, and I pounded his back. My own lungs burned. "You *idiot!*" I raged breathlessly, repeated it in G'mai, then switched to a string of obscenities to rival Gavrin's finest moments. Darik curled, bringing his knees up, and harsh life-giving breath filled his lungs again.

Which meant the pain in my own chest retreated. I bent over him, sea streaming from my hair and clothes, and another chorus of retching went up from the deck. Darik's own tortured heaves were echoed by Gavrin's, and a high-pitched nasal whine that was the yelling of the windwitch D'ri had pulled from the brota's wreck.

Darik sagged against my knees. My arms were afire, clamped as tightly around him as I could manage. "*La'arak, cukrak dihas!*" I swore, over the rising wind and lash of rain pounding the deck. It would sluice the blood away, certainly, and it was near-miraculous they had managed to haul us back onboard. "You should have *told* me!"

It beggared belief that a prince of G'maihallan did not know how to *swim*. If not for shipsick Gavrin disobeying strict orders to stay belowdecks, none would have known the brota had foundered until too late, and little Diyan, disobeying too, would not have plunged into the lashing sea and dragged my *s'tarei* to the surface with a handy shipscrook. The Vulfentown wharf-rat, sleek as a pirifish or an otter and just as at home among the waves, had brought him to the surface, and I fought the sea and the wreckage as well to get us to the side. Gavrin clung to a trailing net, caught the line that had secured the *brota* above, and miraculously forgot his guts heaving out through his mouth long enough to haul us from the Lan'ai's greedy embrace.

The deck spun alarmingly. Lightning sizzle-scorched, a bright silver flash. There was no time to wait for the thunder, not if the battle still raged. Diyan skidded toward me, his dark hair plastered down, my hand shot out and caught his thin arm. "*Stay with him!*" I yelled, gaining my feet in a graceless lunge. Slip-stumbling across the deck, I arrived just in time to see the second corsair, deck alive with flame despite the driving rain, heel desperately away. Those among the *Taryam*'s crew who were still fit for battle let loose a torrent of victory cries, and the last hapless pirate who had clambered onto his deck was swiftly dispatched by the Shainakh *adjii*'s shortblade and tumbled over the side, a loose-jointed doll vanishing into the Lan'ai's hungry mouth.

I stood, sides heaving, dripping and stinging all over. Hrufel, his face slicked with bright blood, started bellowing to check the rigging, and sailors swarmed to obey. The *adjii*, turning from the railing with his dark Shainakh eyes ablaze, raised his shortblade and let out a victory yell that managed to pierce the approaching storm with a bright silver note.

Tyaanismir Atyarik was whole and unharmed, helping Janaire from the captain's deck. He saw me and halted, his face gone soft with shock. Rainak Redfist arrived at my side, giving me a clap on the shoulder that nearly sent me to my knees. "*A fine fight!*" he brayed. "Eh, lass? I have nae wet me axe on a ship before!"

Lucky. So gods-be-damned lucky. I bent over, my belly deep-griping. I heaved a quantity of seawater onto the

29

deck, laced with a goodly amount of sickening white foam, and managed to stagger back for Darik.

Too late. Atyarik and Janaire were already there, the Gavridar *adai*'s hands full of Power as she bent over him. It coruscated from her slim fingers, her travel braids knocked askew but her face alight as she poured healing into him. Diyan crouched beside her, staring adoringly at her soft, set expression.

I found I still had my *dotani*, safe in its sheath, though it would need careful cleaning after this. By all rights, we should not have escaped this lightly.

I shook my head, whipping salt and blood from securely knotted braids. Battle-weariness swamped me, and if not for the sudden sure rasping of instinct along my nerves I might have been too late. A venom-green snake, lying in wait under branches thick with dripping moisture—for a moment I was in the steaming hell of Hachua again, two days into the jungle and I had decided to turn back for Hain before my boots rotted off and the snakes, Mother Moon, the *snakes*—

I tore free of the illusion just in time, my *dotani* flashing down, ringing as it clove air and rain. Steel will banish many types of witchery, and something *inside* me twitched, too, throwing off the poison-spell by mere increments so it splashed harmlessly along the wet deck, smoking but unable to keep its virulence under the double assault of seawater and sky-tears.

The windwitch screamed as I descended upon him, his eyes rolling back in his head, the whites full of the staining of *vavir*-weed. It consumes from the inside out, that dreamy long-stalked herb, and I have heard witches sometimes chew it to gain the future-knowing. Maybe it was why the windwitch was so desperate—it makes you strong, before it eats you—or perhaps we had killed one dear to him in the melee.

Or maybe he simply did not wish to live, hobbled and crippled, slave to the weed or enduring a long agonising death from its lack. His hand jabbed up, hempenwork bracelets clustering both wrists over the blue-black whorls of ink forced under salt-lashed skin. The wind answered, a great gout of seawater foaming over the side, lightning stabbing around the *Taryam*.

I wrenched his head back, my fingers cramping in wooly, matted hair. The *Taryam* shuddered between boiling lightning-lashes, thunder blasting and ripping whatever canvas it could, and a great shuddering swell knocked the ship sideways. Another hungry wave sluiced the back half of the ship, nearly dragging him down, and I worked my knife across the windwitch's throat. A hot spray of blood, his body kicking and flopping uselessly, and I *felt* the life leave him, an ice-scorch brushing my cheeks and wrists and sodden hair.

Knife-work is close, and dirty. And very, very personal.

I dropped the husk, and straightened. Janaire stared, thrown to her knees, Atyarik at her side, bracing his *adai*. Darik lay in their arms, pale as death, coughing and his eyes fever-glittering, and stared as if I were a loathsome creature wriggling under a rock.

After all, I had left my wounded *s'tarei* in the care of strangers, and cut a prisoner's throat right before them. Diyan, sleek and sodden, examined me with bright interest. Of course, he'd probably seen his fair share of throat-cutting in his time, and he probably understood you do not let a *vavir*-stained enemy live.

Of all my companions, the boy perhaps understood me best.

The storm's heaving diminished somewhat. I was right, the windwitch had been urging it on. Had I been a proper *adai* I might have been able to simply halt him, instead of descending to slitting his gills like a common bandit.

I stared at the three G'mai, and they regarded me in turn. I was no *adai*, and now they knew it too. Even D'ri did, I could see as much as his mouth fell open, horror and disgust mingling on his bloody, salt-scoured, pale, outright *beautiful* face.

Too fine for me, no matter what oath he took.

When silence falls inside a sellsword at the end of a battle, none of the outer noises matter so much. I lurched upright, took two steps away from the fresh corpse, and teetered. Across the heaving deck strode Rainak Redfist, his stolid legs adapted with no trouble to riding the sea. *He* did not look disgusted. He simply strolled toward me, bending when he arrived to pick up the lifeless body, meaning to heave it over the side where the Lan'ai could swallow it and be at peace.

I had more in common with a Skaia'lan barbarian and a Vulfentown wharf-rat than with my own kin.

It was high time I remembered as much.

Prize Freedom
More

WE LIMPED INTO ANTAI A tenday later on the wings of the spent storm, almost bare of canvas and every sailor lean as a Hain hunting hound. Since I'd been a-ship so often, I took my turn with the work, glad to have something to fill my hands and drain my head of everything but line, wind, canvas, and wood. We barely escaped another duo of corsair-ships along the chain of small uninhabited islands sheltering Antai from the south, racing up their jagged shorelines with just *barely* enough speed. Kesa of the Swallows Moon Inn had done well in recommending Hrufel, for he was as mad as any who roamed the seas and stubborn as a mountain to boot. Not only that, but there was no attempt to relieve any of his passengers of valuables, no matter how the crew forked an *avert* sign at Janaire *or* eyed Darik's fine clothing. Even Diyan was safe, though I am certain one or two of the crew had tastes that ran to young shipwife. Another proverb: *there is a marrying man on each ship*, said in gutter Shainakh with the syllables for *each ship* twisted halfway to the term they use for boylovers.

The Vulfentown wharf- rat was my companion as I climbed the rigging, quick and nimble as an adolescent feline. I oiled his hands when they cracked under the harsh conditions and sent him below, but after a few hours of snatched rest he would be at it again, scurrying after anything an adult wasn't adroit enough to retrieve, knotting rope with deft little fingers, and simply, generally, making himself useful. Gavrin's shipsickness had vanished after his first taste of open battle and he did his best; Redfist used his bulk to good effect as linchpin during some of the trickier moments.

The G'mai...well. They kept away, especially after I took to sleeping in a battle-dead crewman's hammock instead of their part of the hold. Janaire looked away on those occasions I could not help glancing in her direction, withdrawing behind Atyarik as if she feared my temper. Whenever she came up to deck for a breath of air the crew grumbled, since the sea was angry enough and sight of another witch might roughen her temper even further. D'ri hauled ropes when he was told, and lent what aid he could, and watched me.

At least the ship was small enough he would not fall prey to twinsickness while I avoided him. We were both trapped, and though there is some comfort at not being alone in a cell, most prisoners still prize freedom more.

So, each of us fettered, we scudded over the Lan'ai on the fringes of one storm after another, and had Hrufel not been so adept at his craft we might have ended much further south, maybe even swept out into deeper ocean and dying of thirst on some atoll.

In the end, though, Antai rose on her twelve hills around her gigantic harbor, from crumbling clay of hovel and slum to the garden-cloaked, multicolored stone villas on the heights. Black clouds dropped their curtains behind us, gem-bright lightning tearing rents in the tossing and churning farther out over the depths, but a gleam of setting sun pierced the Lan'ai's distemper and filled the city with gold. A pall of smokesteam lay cupped in the counting-bowl, a reek of commerce along the quays and docks, counting-houses and open-air markets teeming all day and most of the night as well.

Coin does not sleep, Antai says, *unless it has a lazy owner.* Laziness is the worst insult that can be flung at a native of the Lan'ai Antaihu, the Westron Rim. Their nobles do not shrink at turning a profit, like those among the Shainakh who consider *business* a blot upon the family honor. You can buy a title in Antai—or twelve of them, if you prefer, along with sinecures and interests and a crumbling villa certified to be old as the city itself. Or older, depending on whose arse you oil for the right collection of seals and ribbons.

The very southron end of the territory the Anhedrin—for so the natives of the Westron Rim call themselves, a word that means "travelers" in their hinterland tongue—lay claim to ends on the barren, blasted Kavakh peninsula some few days' journey from the great city itself, where the last Khana Alhai of the Pensari was said to have cut his own throat with a curse rather than be taken captive by a ragtag army of slave-rebels. Antai remembers that it was the great mass of her lowest scum who drove him there, rising in rebellion. Some of Antai's oldest families claim descent from the Pensari's pale night-worshipping legions, but not very loudly. Some even say the Clau, those ghost-skinned island folk, are related to them.

The Clau have their own legends and witchery, but they do not share either. Even Kesa did not speak much of her homeland, not even in her bed.

"Never thought I'd see this again," Redfist said beside me, his odorous bulk looming. He was pale too, though his ruddiness would save him from suspicion of Pensari blood.

"You came through Antai?" My voice cracked from disuse—there had not been much to say, except brief yells warning another sailor of some danger, or of my intentions so they could leave me to my work.

"Aye. Took the Pass south from Karnagh, once I was out of irons." He glared at the city as if it had personally offended him. "Dunkast never expected some might actually be loyal to their own kin, the bastard."

I absorbed this. Citynoise bounced over the water, reflecting oddly from a liquid mirror—chantsong from heaving laborers, ringing gongs and bells from the temples, shrieking and bleating from the animal pens, the din of humanity. After so long with merely waves, wind, and our own thoughts, it was an assault, and one I welcomed. The work of landfall would delay the inevitable confrontation with the G'mai. "Where is Karnagh?"

"North. At the throat of the Pass, but first ye have to pass through the demon's arsehole." He looked very much as if he wanted to spit, his coppery eyebrows knotting together.

"*Demon's arsehole*? Is that like *red-eyed bugger*?"

That earned me an amused glance. "*That* was a figure o'speech, lass."

At least he had not lost his humor.

"Do you ever long for home?" It was the first time I ever asked directly, and perhaps the wrong moment, because he said nothing, simply continued gazing at the hills, the rich merchants' houses called *earthfoam* because they were cast to the top of the land-swells. Gulls coasted, their thin piping cries drowned out as we drifted into the distress channel, waiting our turn. Our battered state would be easy enough to spot from shore, a pilot and heaver were already scrambling from one of the outer docks. At least Hrufel's cargo was safe; he would realize a healthy profit from this voyage even if he had to repair a good bit of canvas and scrape the *Taryam*'s hull. There was also the last half of the passage fee Kesa had negotiated for us, and I added another ten silver sequins atop it, perhaps because I was exhausted enough to be charitable, and perhaps because his men had treated me no differently than any other sailor. Most of the crew would winter here, I suspected, since the season was already turning.

What I would not have given to be one of them. And yet.

Ammerdah Rikyat had expected to winter in Shaitush. The thought was a pinch in a sore spot.

My luck will turn against me, Kaia!

Hrufel's *adjii* bellowed from the captain-deck, and I turned to helping the *Taryam* dress himself for company.

THE NUMBER
MAKES HIM UNEASY

TO WALK ON LAND AFTER crossing the Lan'ai is...disconcerting. The sea hides in your legs and bones and breath, and the earth pitches under you strangely by not moving at all. Arriving at dusk as a storm threatened from the Shelt meant the inns on the lower slopes were bursting with cutpurses and the like, as well as raucous sailors delayed by tide and wind. Up the hills, then, stepping carefully alongside a cart pulled by an ill-tempered roan nag and holding Diyan, the minstrel—who looked green again—and Janaire, who pulled up the hood of her salt-stained travel cloak and bowed her dark head, sitting on the locked chest containing most of Ammerdahl Rikyat's blood-gold gift. Atyarik paced on the other side, glaring at any who dared press too closely, Darik followed me, and Redfist brought up the rear of our strange little column. The driver tried to cheat me on the price of cartage, but I swore at him in half-Pesh tradetongue and he sighed, spreading his nimble paws as if to say *well, this is Antai, one must try.*

Night thickened in every corner, whistles and streetstall calls giving way to lantern-bearers crying their ancient ululating chorus, and we crossed the Atluah—the great sea-curving avenue that bisects Antai from north to south—twice before the packed-close structures began to draw apart, allowing a little air between their walls. Weariness filled every part of me, and more than once I considered sinking down onto the filthy street and simply letting the world pass for a little while.

Consequently, when we arrived at a handsome whitewashed inn with a colonnaded front and supercilious stable-boys, my temper was none too sweet. I almost cuffed one of the brats who scurried out to tell us the inn was full, and stamped up the three steps for the carven front door. The sign bore red grapes and a running white horse, freshly painted every summer, and the doorguard was new—a stocky part-Hain who leveled his much-oiled blackstick across the entrance and eyed me from top to toe with what I am certain he thought was stinging disdain.

It turned to dignified attention when I showed a silver Hain sequin and told him to send for his master, for Kaia Steelflower had returned.

That widened his narrow Hainish eyes, and he waved the stable-brats away from our cart, sending an attendant into the depths of the inn. I considered sitting on the steps, but if I did, I would not rise before I had slept enough, and Thanourt did not take kindly to beggars fouling his precious columns. *Real Clau marble,* he would preen, at least once every drinking-session. *Do you know what that costs?*

No doubt he did, down to the last copper bit. I did not have the heart to tell him that they looked like polished Pesh quarry-blocks. But I am no stonewright, and far be it for a sellsword to rob an innkeeper of his prickly pride.

As if the thought of copper bits had summoned him, a blur of bleached apron and wide black moustache weighted with red clay beads that clacked as he grinned wide and white and vicious appeared. "Ah, so sorry—" he began, bowing, his gaze passing right over me as if I was not one of his regular customers, whenever I passed through Antai.

Of course, I would hardly recognise myself when I came offship after such a passage, but one expects an innkeeper to be a little better at it.

My hold on my temper frayed, but did not snap completely. "Three rooms and a bathing suite, Nansou ak'Thanourt, and our board as well, for at least a sevenday. Or I shall set fire to your inn and melt your marble columns." My braids were crust-glued to my head, I ached in every bone, and I was abruptly aware that I stank of ship, as no doubt everyone but Janaire did.

A real *adai*, of course, could use Power to cleanse the travel-weariness away.

"Is that..." He blinked in the dusk, and the doorguard lifted a hastily kindled lanthorn. "By Rheldakh's Seven Teats, it *is* you! I shall take the skin off that brat's back for not telling me—come, come, Kaia, and I will not charge you more than seven silvers a day!"

"Three," I spat, but I extended my hands and we gripped wrists as friends in that thieving city do—to keep each other from picking their pockets, as the proverb goes. "And don't forget the bath."

"Ai, Kaia-*hanua*, what is that? A giant? Five silver, and copper for every hundredweight the giant eats!"

For the love of the gods... I swallowed an obscenity often heard shipside when a sailor has crowded too close again and again. "Five it is, no more, and if you don't mind your tongue I'll set the Northerner upon *you*. His axe was exercised on a dozen-and-one pirates during our crossing, and the number makes him uneasy."

Redfist glowered magnificently through his salt-whitened beard, and Thanourt actually paled a bit, which ignited a weary sort of cheer behind my breastbone. I did not sway on my feet only through sheer force of will, and we slapped hands to seal the bargain. I paid him half with the leftover break-bits from the passage-fee, and left the unloading of the cart to the rest of my little band of outcasts. I had brought them to this harbor, as safely as I could manage.

"And you will be wanting news, Kaia." Thanourt gestured me inside.

"Yes, but not now." I could ignore Darik, I found, as long as I was exhausted enough not to feel his presence— or the lack of it. The lower commonroom passed in a blur of smoke, mead-smell, and voices; I followed Thanourt up familiar stairs that did not slide so much underfoot as leap randomly from one point to the next. I took the room furthest from the bathing-suite, and told him what I wanted. He nodded, stroking his beard. It was a nervous motion, and my weary cheer turned to consciousness of the various nips and gnawing all over me. Sellswords are hardy, but ever since Hain I felt the invisible hand of age upon me, bone to joint.

You have not given yourself much rest, a small voice whispered in the back of my head. It sounded suspiciously like Darik's, struggling through a wall of formless noise that blurred every nuance. Was he trying to speak-within to me?

It didn't matter. Not now. "Thanourt?"

He turned back, his eyebrows raising, and there were gray and silver threads in his black beard. His beaded and oiled moustache held no trace of time's pale feathering, but there were white wires in his fine mop of dark hair, too. He had softened about the belly and the shoulders, though there was still good muscle under the padding. I had thought him a giant, before I met Redfist; Thanourt was nothing beside the ruddy barbarian's bulk.

"It's...good to see you," I managed, awkwardly. "Take care with my companions."

"Ai, of course, Kaia!" He bowed, without any of a merchant's flourishes, and I noticed what I should have

41

first—the leather braces at his wrists were gone, the scars underneath now on display. The marks had somewhat faded, and no longer reddened with his exertions up the stairs. "They shall be treated well in this inn, and they shall be singing praises of my hospitality from here to..." He waited, to see if I would give any indication of my bearings after this port.

I treated him to the most genuine smile I could manage with a weariness-frozen face. Even my ears hurt, to their very tips. My toes each sang an individual song of stiff, cramped pain.

"Do not send so much as a maid to this door until I open it again," I repeated, and slammed the heavy oak. There was no bar, merely a lock, and I turned it without caring much that it was flimsy protection at best. No fire, but there was a bed wide enough for two if they did not mind closeness, and a small window with heavy shutters that would have shown me the inner courtyard and the cook's garden, if I cared to look.

I tacked unevenly across the floor, almost tripping on one of the Trejan rugs, and fell face-first upon the prettily made bed. I did not take off my weapons, or my boots, or anything else.

Instead, I fell into a dark well of sleep, still feeling the ship's creaking underneath...

...and wishing, as I had for days now, for the steady warmth of a G'mai *s'tarei* beside me.

A Little Sour

THE EMPEROR HAD, AFTER ALL, *taken this rebellion seriously. They came around the southron hill, the real bulk of the army, not the Hamashaüken advance-guard. The head of their column should not have outpaced the main body so far, but the Emperor's Elect were arrogant, believing in their nickname—the Immortals. The shield-fist of Empire, as the Blue Hand was the shadowed, knife-bearing other arm.*

From above, it unfolds as if in a teaching-tale, one of the classic battles warmasters draw in sand with sticks, or move colored counters upon a painted board to represent. The rebels, taking trophies and administering mercy-blows, were caught in the open, struggling to reform their line. Choking dust rose in veils, and one wing of cavalry charged, wheeling about the flank of the scattered rebel forces. They would later fall upon the baggage-train, the camp and its followers, and take their fill of plunder twice-won.

They said he had the favor of the gods, this one. There had even been...distressing signs. Droughts, the great blood-soaked morass of the Danhai war adding to public restlessness, and the priestesses of the harvest goddess had withdrawn from certain public festivals—and now this upstart, claiming to speak for the War God himself.

The War God did not stretch forth his hand to cover his chosen upon that day.

A one-handed general on an ill-tempered stallion managed to rally a group around the pretender in the saddle between the two hills, and they stood firm through three infantry charges. Their banner, a proud white horse, hangs limp and tattered, but still upright. The rabble in the rebel army melts away, screaming and dropping armor and weapons, ridden down from behind. It is a coney-catch, and few escape.

Only the fanatic and the desperate are left, those who truly believe and those who will not be pardoned if they do somehow survive. Dust, bowel-stink, and blood mix into mud around their boots.

From above, the end is never in question, only how long. After the third cavalry charge, the thunder of nailed boots crests, and the fresh, eager infantry break upon the rebels like a wave. Kevest One-Hand, bleeding from four mortal wounds and roaring the name of his ill-tempered white horse, falls. Shammardine Taryana fights until she is spitted on a peasant conscript's pike, probably raging at the daring of such a lowborn.

Surrounded, the pretender does not waste time. He knows they will take him alive if they can, to be paraded on an open cart through the capital city, then caged in the Emperor's rain-garden as he starves to death. The pretender has set the hilt of a shortsword against a handy rock at the side of the road, his Danhai longblade dropped into the dust, and before he casts himself upon the blade he looks up, as if he can see me.

Ammerdahl Rikyat's face is a mask, and he pitches forward, one last convulsive movement—

...straight into sitting up, despite the scream of protest from every stiffened muscle, a full chant-chorus like the groups of gelded boys the Hain are rumored to have singing for their Empress night and day to keep her young. My left hand was full of knifehilt, my right in a bruising-hard grip around a thin wrist, and I almost plunged the blade into flesh before I realized who, and where, and *what* I was.

The nightmare-cry died in my throat, an inelegant croak. Little Diyan stared at me, his big dark eyes shining. He didn't look in the least frightened. He was even freshly washed, the festival-day shirt and breeches bought for him before we boarded the *Taryam* rumpled but much better than the ragged mess his clothes had become aboard. Thin spears of gray daylight fingered the shutters, and a clay lamp full of clarified khafish-oil burned low on the table, its flame blue at its heart and thankfully not reeking of oceandweller's guts.

"Mother's *tits*," I rasped, "how did *you* get in?"

Then I realized I'd spoken in G'mai, and it was an effort to shift to tradetongue. "Diyan. How did you get in?" I let go of his shirt-front slowly, my knife sliding back into its home.

He beamed. "Better locks in Vulfentown, *cha*. You slept two days."

"I believe it." I rubbed at my face—saltglaze crackled free, and every inch of skin I possessed itched. My feet ached too, trapped and swollen in stiffened bootleather. The dream revolved inside my skull, refusing to settle in sleep's lurid-colored but ultimately illusory country. I could still hear the screaming. "What of the others, little one?"

"Barbarian's in commonroom with dice, minstrel went to temple." The irreligious little wharf-rat made a scornful face, though Gavrin was probably right to offer thanks for our arrival to any god he chose. "Prettywitch and longface are with D'ri. Are you still *a-thatch* at all'n?"

"They are more *thatch'n* with me, small one. Let me see your hands."

He held them up, little capable paws crosshatched with pink and white rope-marks. A flicker around his fingertips told me Janaire was still applying healings to him, even without my asking.

Among the G'mai, children are cherished, even flawed ones. It had been...difficult, when I left the borders of my homeland, to understand the sheer number of cast-away little ones, prey to slavers and others of darker purpose. In

Kar-Amyus I had even seen the corpse of a boy of no more than six summers beaten to death by his own kin.

Such things do not become easier to witness, no matter how common. Kar-Amyus had taught me much, though I could not have returned the favor. One young half-starved sellsword is not enough to leave a mark upon an entire city.

"*You're* th'thatch'n, K'li." He handled the stop in the diminutive well. "D'ri keeps back an forth, ox grinding corn. No talk, no eating. Longface says you goan kill him."

I tested his fingers—no loss of flexibility. He would be none the worse for his shipboard stubbornness. And Darik was pacing. "Kill Atyarik? Why?"

"No. D'ri."

I would sooner cut my own hand off. I shook my head, muscles in my neck protesting afresh. The times when I could simply sleep away crossing the Lan'ai were gone. Even G'mai feel time's kiss, and a sellsword's life does not make for comfort in one's old age—assuming one is lucky enough to reach that far. How many times had I simply laid the question of my own survival aside?

Now my own life was not mine to waste as I saw fit.

I contented myself with shaking my aching, filthy head. "Have you eaten, little one?"

"Oh, *cha*. Big table. Fat man says you took him up-coffle. Tha'so?"

So Thanourt was telling the story again. The wagon, the filthy straw, the clinking sound. The slave-chains, and the mud, and the guttural screams as my blade plunged deep into a fat belly.

Traveling brings you to strange companions, and some of them were not nearly as well-mannered as G'mai, a wharf-rat, a barbarian, and a Pesh lutebanger. I wondered how Gavrin's instrument had fared during its sea-crossing.

I contented myself with ruffling Diyan's hair. "You are an *inquisitive* little creature."

He ducked away, with a shy smile. He was young, yes, but already learning the diffidence of adolescents. "Listening don' cost nuffink, *cha*?"

"*Cha*," I agreed, deciding not to tell a tale where an eavesdropper lost his life. There are many, and none of them fit for a child's ears. Even if the child had probably seen more of life's underside than many an adult of more tender environs. "Now, little one, I am bound for the bath. Run and tell the innkeep I've awakened, and will expect a meal. Gods above, what time is it?"

"Just past nooning." He slid off the bed, raking his hair back with quick fingers. Barefoot, he stepped carefully, and he would, in time, make a very fine thief. Perhaps I should apprentice him to someone in the city? "Kaia?"

"Hm?" I bent to my boots. Getting them off suddenly seemed the most important matter in the world.

"Are you gon' kill D'ri?"

Why does he ask again? What has he been told? "Of course not. Why do you ask?"

"He look fair maund." With a flick of his capable paws and a heave at the door, he was gone into the hall. My skin crawled, my bones ached, and the consciousness of every problem looming before me turned to cold, heavy metal against my shoulders and my throbbing neck.

"A bath," I muttered. "Whatever happens, let me be clean."

I worked my boots off and trudged for the fallwater, shedding filthy cloth as I went, and hoping against hope I would be granted a little peace before I faced one of the G'mai.

My luck, however, was still a little sour.

MADE OF
YOUR METAL

THE BATHING-SUITE HELD TWO tubs—one tepid, one steaming, and I wanted a bath hot as wingwyrm breath. Unfortunately, the steam parted to reveal long dark hair ravelling on the water's surface and the tips of dainty ears poking shyly through the dark silk, and Janaire's sweet lowland face peered at me.

In the mountains, the temperament as well as the appearance of my folk is sharper, bred of the bones of the earth and the wind that scours bare rock. Lowlanders are held to be less dour, and in them the beauty and the pride of Mother Moon's chosen people becomes a *kymiri* blossom dipped in filigree, its blurred fragility on display in an imperishable casing. She smiled, like dawn breaking over the rolling hills of the river-country, and a swift pang went through me. Battered and scarred, my feet gnarled from boots and muscle in flat straps and sheathes all over me dispelling any female softness, I was a damaged dish next to her, and well I knew it.

She did not seem to care, but those with beauty can afford to be generous. Gavridar Janaire was everything I would never be, and I could not even hate her. She carried out her duties as a potential *Yada'Adais* with fierce dedication, though I was an unruly student at best, and my sharpness seemed more likely to wound her than to strike an answering spark.

It was always and ever the same. Years of navigating the world alone had turned me into a collection of edges, each sharper than the last, and those who brushed against me were lucky to escape scarring.

"Kaia!" She even *sounded* happy to see me, curse her. "You're awake."

Her lowlander accent turned the words to a lullaby. Outsiders have much difficulty with our language—the inflections sound similar to ears not born and bred to them.

I glanced at the tepid pool, braced myself, and found the shallow steps into the hot one. Warm water enveloped me, the waves of my entrance lapping against her. Her cheeks were rosy; she had been soaking for some time.

Good. She would perhaps be done soon.

"How do you feel?" She moved, lazily, and made her own ripples, canceling mine as soon as they met. She could no doubt shape the steam any way she wished, or draw the heat from the water with a word, capable of working what other folk called witchery but to us is as natural as breathing.

Since leaving G'maihallan, I avoided witches of any kind. We make each other...uncomfortable. Now I wondered if they could sense the Power in me, dammed up and swelling like sealed woundrot, when I had not been able to sense it myself.

I found my voice with an effort. "Well enough, *adai'sa*. Thank you." I found the proper formal inflection, I the lowly student and she a full-fledged Teacher. The cadence of G'mai was a thorny pleasure after so long with tradetongue and the slang, loan-words, and mess of every other language.

"Good, good." She paused, and the blush in her cheeks was not merely heat.

Oh, Mother Moon. What now?

"I must broach a delicate matter," she said, formally, and she was *still* using the wrong inflection—as if I were an older agemate of hers, and due respect. "Will you give me leave to do so, Anjalismir Kaia?"

"I can hardly stop you." It sounded ill-tempered, and uttered in common besides.

She kept to G'mai, and kept the inflection. "Your *s'tarei...*"

I said nothing. Settled on the bathing-bench, wood instead of stone but quite serviceable. The heat would work inward, dispelling muscle aches. Were I alone, I would be contemplating a walk to the Bathai Temple, to see if Manil Kasoua was still among the flesh-kneaders there. She was an old woman, and half-blind, but her fingers were iron.

And even if she was not still kneading the aches of those who visited the Antai god called the Mender of Ills, she was...friendly enough. Any kneader at the temple would have the latest news.

So would Thanourt. He would no doubt dole out a serving of it with my meal, if I had any stomach left after this conversation.

"Kaia...Has he displeased you?"

The term she used was uncomfortably precise—*k'din'jasa*, the inflection lifting the second-to-last syllable, implying a well-deserved banishment from a refuge. The word for a *s'tarei* treading the edge of being outcaste.

Bath-heat worked inward. My legs relaxed, the knotted muscles in my thighs finally loosening. "He is the one displeased." I shut my eyes, my head finding a scallop in the rim of the tub. It held the back of my skull comfortably enough, and I let out an involuntary sigh. "I left him during a battle."

"Ah. Well." She cleared her throat, a small uncomfortable sound. "We have been...there is disagreement. The prince says he should have killed the foreign witch instead of forcing his *adai* to such a measure. I have said the fault is mine, for not recognising the danger, and my *s'tarei* has been determined to take it upon himself, for not striking down a threat to the prince and the prince's *adai*." She sighed again, a long, drawn-out sound. Perhaps she had been waiting in this tub for too long. "I do not know, Anjalismir Kaia." Unbearably formal, her inflection. "I simply wish...will you not speak to your *s'tarei*? And to the rest of us?" *Now* she switched to tradetongue, and her grasp of it was markedly improved. "Your silence, it is...cold."

"There was not time to speak." It felt like a halt, lame imposter of an excuse, and it was. "There was only survival."

"Oh, aye." Did she sound sarcastic, or merely weary? "We are not all made of your metal, *Steelflower*." The inflection made them the name out of words for brittle metal and a starflower, those cold-loving early-blooming, brief splashes of color announcing winter's hold was slipping but not broken.

We are addicted to wordplay, we Children of the Moon, and I had not thought her quite so handy with it. It was not the first, or the last, time Gavridar Janaire surprised me.

"Tis probably a good thing, Yada'Adais." I half closed my eyes. A teacher of Power is much respected in G'maihallan, and even their insults are borne with grace. Though rare indeed was a Yada'Adais who stooped to *insult*.

They have other means of making any displeasure felt.

Ripples and currents touched me as she glided smoothly for the steps, a Lan'ai in miniature. Heat shimmered along my skin, worked into every pore and crevice, and once she was gone I could soak-bake my body and conscience at the same time.

"Atyarik is right," she said as she lifted herself from the water's embrace. Her supple, pale back bore no stripe or scar, and the curve of her hips was not yet in its full ripeness. She was a girl, still. And far from home.

I did not ask what her *s'tarei* was right about. I suspected she would tell me, and I was proven correct.

"You *will* kill him." Flatly, and with terrible certainty, as she wrapped herself in a bathing-robe, her hair a river of molten darkness. "Because he came too late, and you will not forgive that, any more than you forgave your warlord friend for his lies."

There is a point past which pain becomes indistinguishable from heat. I stayed in the bath for a half-candlemark after, pulling the chain once for more hot water. Nobody else came to disturb me, and I was glad, because the wetness on my cheeks could not be blamed on the steam.

MUCH TO CHEW

SCRUBBING AND A LONG HOT soak will give a weary sellsword's body much less of the ship-creak. It also tangles hair, if you are foolish enough not to close-crop like a Pesh bondslave. Working through the mass with a comb and two picks required patience and a palmful or two of cras-oil, the fragrant pressing of the white meat of a brown hairy fruit that ripens slowly but in prodigious quantities. Brought up the trade-routes from Pesh, it is not overly expensive in Antai as long as the summer has been good. It does not become rancid, and one can eat it, cook with it, and rub it into hair and body at will. The Pesh, in their city of dust and caged flames, even burn cras as fuel.

I wondered if the scent would cause Gavrin a pang. The lash cuts deep, and even if the scar heals, it still...echoes.

I settled on the bed, cross-legged, wondering if I wished for more sleep instead of dinner. The table in my room was laid for two, but it was not Thanourt who appeared as I finished the work of braiding and looping, my fingers making their quick habitual movements as I gazed at thick diamond-panes of amber-tinted glass. Late-summer sun filled them with fire, but the light had the sharp edge of almost-harvest. Winter would arrive soon, but I had brought them all, every one of them, safely to Antai.

At least I had accomplished *one* thing I had set myself to lately.

I heard his step in the hall, and braced myself. By the time he tapped at the door I was even able to say "Enter," without the word sticking in my throat. It was only then I realized I spoke in G'mai, the sharp syllables giving polite permission. In a land where every inhabitant has some measure of Power, granting others a privacy is a necessity. Was it his heart beating quickly in my own chest and wrists? At least ship-work and exhaustion had meant I could not tell if the pain was his or mine, I simply endured it.

Every journey has a stop, whether it be camp, or waystation, or city. Every stop means there may be time to think. Or to answer questions.

"Kaia." Quietly, as he closed the door. Black silk and leather, the cut different than any cloth in the markets of Antai or anywhere else on the Rim, allowing freedom of movement in equal measure to grace. His hand dropped— he had just pushed his hair back from his eyes, a short irritable motion that still held a great deal of fluidity.

"Darik." I tied the last bit of ship's twine in a lover's knot, its roughness against my callused fingertips a scraping reminder that a true G'mai girl would have a pretty ribbon or two to hold her braids steady. Janaire certainly did.

"Are you well?" Eyes so dark pupil and iris blended. Not like my own golden gaze. The Moon's children are night-dark in hair and eye; light irises are not quite common, and a little suspect.

I had often thought it a mark of my flaws. The only G'mai woman lacking Power, lacking the Moon's gifts, the proper birthright of every *adai*, walking alone while the rest...Well. He had arrived, and everything had changed, and now I could lose him between one breath and the next. A moment's carelessness could founder us both.

We are born to the twinning, and do not survive its breaking. Once, perhaps, in the very first days of bonding.

Not anymore.

"Are *you*?" Tradetongue made my mouth and lips feel too thick. I forced myself to think in the trade-pidgin, not the sharp lilting beauty of G'mai.

"Well enough." He held himself tall and tense, shoulders rigid under black cloth. His clothing, altogether fine enough for a traveling princeling, was mended with expert, tiny stitches. Probably Janaire's, since my needlework was fine enough for split flesh or coarse sellsword's shirt and jerkin. Not nearly enough, though, for an exquisite mending of subtly patterned G'mai silk and linen, not to mention leather.

"Then I am, as well." I tried a smile. It sat unnaturally on my frozen face. "Shall you be dining with me, princeling?"

"If it pleases you."

My hands dropped too, loose and useless now that my hair was braided and coiled. No rope to catch, no canvas to check or mend, no salt-scoured wood to clutch, no pitching and tossing underfoot to fight. Just one G'mai sellsword facing a battle she did not want.

There were battles one could crave, in youth or fury. They grow rarer, the longer a sellsword survives.

My tentative smile fell away, and we studied each other in a small Antai innroom, the fire speaking its subtle language of light, heat, and ash.

"You do not have to," I said, finally.

"What if I wish to?" He did not move. I knew he would not raise his voice, or attempt to strike me—a *s'tarei* simply does not do such things.

Still, I was unprepared for him to be this...this *calm.* "Why would you wish to?" I finally flung the words at him. "I left your side during a battle, Dragaemir. I am no *adai.*"

He shook his head, once, a graceful negation. Indicated the table with a brief gesture, as if inviting me to sit. "I am a fool. That is all."

A cold wind began in the center of my bones. I set my jaw, swallowed a heavy bitterness. "Do you wish me to return your *dauq'adai?*" The Seeker lay, its gem a colorless brightness, under my much-mended shirt and my second jerkin as well, supple leather hanging loosely on me now. There are words for a *s'tarei* flung from the grace of the twinning, but none for an *adai's* fall. The bearers of life and Power are simply too precious to contemplate mistreating. Even I, born flawed, had been cared for.

Darik simply regarded me. "Kaialitaa." Very softly, the purest G'mai sending a spike through my chest, lingering on my name to turn it into an endearment, *little brave one.* "I will have no other *adai.* Is that clear enough to penetrate even *your* stubborn skull?"

"Why?" My hands had folded into fists. "I am a *disappointment*, Darik."

"To whom?" The inquiry, given in such a tone of mild interest, hung lightly in the room. He crossed to the window, long efficient strides, as the sunlight drained from the glass. His boots were just as scarred as my own, now, and probably still held traces of the Lan'ai. Other than that, and his leanness, he was unmarked by the passage.

Must you make me say it? The thought leapt from my consciousness to his, the voice-within so long denied it almost hurt. "You."

"Am I allowed my own feelings on the matter, *adai'mi?*"

My hands had turned to fists. He stared at the panes, his dark hair damp and brushed back. Was the pain in my chest his, or mine?

"Of course." I denied the urge to stand, the urge to touch a knifehilt. I sat perfectly still, braced for disaster again. "I would like to know those feelings."

"Look, and find out." *Do I need to say it again, Kaia?* The voice-within allows for nuances, shadings, that speech cannot hold. His anger would have hurt me less than the wash of pure, clean warmth, the tenderness blooming along an invisible cord stretched between us.

"Perhaps I need to *hear* it." Why were six small words, delivered in soft, almost lisping G'mai—because my lips were numb—so difficult? My stomach twinged, hunger returning now that I was clean and there was a chance of my belly being filled. Nothing is as sharp as the emptiness that sees it might soon be satisfied.

"I had lost all hope." He spoke softly, in G'mai, and the *dauq-adai* warmed against my breastbone. It had been fading when I'd picked it out of Redfist's pocket, a cheap streetseller's gaud, but now...

Now it was completely different. Everything was.

"You are my *adai*. Not even the Moon Herself could make me turn from you." He nodded, sharply, and turned from the window to regard me, chin set, eyes ablaze, the very picture of a *s'tarei*. He was too fine for an innroom. Too fine to be dragged along a sellsword's life, from one mouthful to the next, gnawing hunger in the belly and the chaos of battle ringing in the head. "*In'sh'tai.*"

So it is.

We watched each other for a long breathless moment. A soft rap at the door broke the headwaters of whatever river had gathered inside me—it was Thanourt, bustling in with the first of many lacquered trays in his beefy paws, the smell of *chaabi* stew suddenly overpowering. Behind him, two inngirls peeped through the door, and cautiously entered with the wine-jugs and another tray.

"Ah, Iron Flower! I bring you much to chew." Thanourt did not bow, but he inclined his upper half a little, rounding his shoulders. Perhaps I was the only one who could see the almost-flinch. The body never forgets, once the collar has been pinned shut and the coffle begins to move.

By the end of a slave's first day, iron has stamped the spine into a curve.

"Thanourt, my friend." I rose, wincing a bit as my lower back reminded me I had spent too many nights sleeping in a swaying clump of netting. "Is that *chaabi* I smell? What news do you bring me?" The peculiar slur and lift of Antai's tradespeech takes a little while to fit in the mouth properly, but once it does, one never loses it. It is a division of common that flows and changes more than any other place's except perhaps Shaituh, that navel of a great empire sinking under its own weight.

"Oh, there's much afoot," he said, cheerfully. "Perhaps I shall drink a cup with you and your *hasti* there, and tell you all, were I invited?"

Hasti? Who told him I was married? To deny it would only cause a need for explanation. "You need no invitation, tis your own wine."

"True enough, but better with friends." His quick, broad-palmed hands soon had the table set to rights, and Darik drifted closer, pausing at the foot of the bed. How could a princeling look so uncertain?

I beckoned, indicating the other seat with what I hoped was good grace. "Sit. Thanourt's *chaabi* is famous. Unless he's rid himself of that ill-tempered cook."

The innkeep threw up both hands, an exuberant Antai gesture. "Alas, I cannot. I married him. He sends his regards, and tells you he did *not* spit in your soup."

The cook Senpha Subo, former thief and master of many a kitchen, had once threatened to poison me if I caused Thanourt grief, and I thought it likely there was an attraction between them. "No extra flavour for me, then." An unwilling laugh forced its way free of my throat. The inngirls—one Pesh-fair, one Shainakh dark with the proud nose of a full blood— both gazed at me with open-mouth wonder. "Tell me, young ones, does Nansou-kin here treat you well?"

They blushed, and the Shainakh girl dropped her gaze and almost the wine bottles. The Pesh, though, gave me a pert little wink and a broad smile that showed a missing canine. The other was pearly, and very sharp. "Ay he does, Kahaai Iron-petal. What we din'eat go straight to the hog, and not the other way turned."

It wasn't so much what she said—it was a passable enough jest—as it was the broad Shainakh accent.

Kahaai. In the slang of the Shainakh irregulars, it meant a balky mare, and many had been the laugh at a particular couplet or two likening me to one during the Danhai campaign. It reminded me of Ammerdahl Rikyat, and the dream.

I do not have the future-dreaming. It was only my fears, and exhaustion, and a bad sea-crossing.

"Kaia?" Darik took another step forward, and Thanourt was eyeing me curiously as well, shooing the girls out to bring yet more covered dishes up for our repast and a chair for his own oddly graceful bulk.

"Nothing." I shook my head, the heaviness on my shoulders not merely the weight of the braids atop my head. "Come, Thanourt, and pour the wine." I was clean, and rested, and an ocean away from the man who sought to use me; I had brought my troupe safely to the closest thing to a home I had in Antai.

I should have known it wouldn't be enough.

59

What Is Owed

A GOOD *CHAABI* STEW IS savoury-sweet, just enough heat to make the throat sing and the eyes prickle, but not enough to make either weep. The meat is tender, long-simmered, but the meatroots must still have some tooth left in them and the balance of spices must be smoky and deep, with layers like a good Quort wine. Thanourt's husband was a marvelous cook, and though his *chaabi* was not as sublime as Kesa's, it was still a work of art, and a reminder that I had survived yet another crossing of the Shelt's dangerous blue depths. Two kitchens, divided by water, and should I settle someday with my own inn I would have time to perfect my own *chaabi*. Tis said to be one of the Four Recipes a cook can spend a lifetime inching towards mastery of.

Perhaps it was a foolish sellsword's dream, but it was mine. Six rooms for guests, seven waterclosets, linens hung in the sun. I would be the one passing news to weary travelers and bargaining with tax collectors. I could not imagine a Dragaemir condescending to such a thing, though. And had I really expected to save enough to buy an inn? Water flows through a sellsword's hands, and so does money. Replacing gear when one has to leave a city quickly, or making caches, are both expensive as a R'jiin courtesan's favors.

In Antai they do not serve the courses as the Free Cities and Shainakh do. First there is the hearty fare, then there is fruit of other small sweet things, and there is no *piri* sauce to be found, only semi-sweet *havaou* to douse crumbling white cheese on flatbread for an appetizer.

I set to with flatbread, eating picks, and a will, and Thanourt began with taxes, with Antai news, and some few hangings or imprisonments. Some of the Thieves' Guild had been a little less than circumspect lately, and the Pesh merchants were nervous. Which led to the Dokka and the Guard lacking even a hint of a sense of humor, or propriety.

Of course one can't have too many thieves running about, Thanourt remarked, *but really, their Guild works hard, too. No better investor than the head of that Guild, they say.*

I could have agreed, but I let Thanourt tell me. The Guild doesn't speak of its business to innkeepers. It is an ancient and honorable institution, and has spread its tentacles far. Any trouble with local Guard or governor was a matter of finding the right pressure to apply to return the world to equilibrium.

Or the right throat to cut. I was halfway through my second bowl of *chaabi* and my third glass of tart, sweet Kshanti white wine before the scope of the conversation widened.

The innkeeper settled, folding his capacious hands. He even left scrapings in the bottom of his lacquerware bowl, to show his husband he was not hungry. He wore no band around his first left finger, but now I could see the chain about his neck. Finemetal, thin and beautiful, and it probably held the contract-ring. "Old Golden-Arse is gone mad, they say. Sent two of his nephews and three of his concubines to the chopping block." Thanourt sighed. "The Pesh were hoping he'd forget his expansion dreams, but now that he's put that rebellion down—"

I set my bowl down. "Rebellion?" Old news to me, but...*put the rebellion down?*

"Ahi-ya, a good one, too. Twas said even the harvest goddess was behind him, but women are fickle always." Thanourt smiled, stroking his moustache, smoothing the mellow clay beads. D'ri glanced at me, and it was some small comfort to see he'd laid aside some of his exquisite palace manners and lifted his bowl like a sellsword, shoveling the *chaabi* down with all due speed and a scallop of flatbread. "Even you, Kaia-*hanua.*"

"A sellsword can't afford to be too rigid," I returned. "The sea is changeable, and she a woman too."

"At least you admit it."

I shook my head, hefting my goblet. If he was about to tell me what I suspected he was, I would need it. The wine poured down, cool and crisp and utterly ineffectual. "So, a rebellion."

"Led by some petty noble who survived the second season of Danhai. Some said he won a battle, then lost one. Either way, his corpse was carted back to Shaitush for the cage, they say."

My stomach turned over, the *chaabi* briefly rising from its intended home. I breathed out, then in, forcing food and wine back down into my cellar. "I thought they only did that to live criminals."

"Well, old Golden-Arse wanted him brought back either way. Ah, here's the ciri-fruit! A good harvest this year, and I have darkhoney from Clau. Subo has something special in mind for it."

"The mead will be very fine," I replied, numbly. Darik lowered his bowl, and his dark gaze had grown sharp. He did not miss much, the Heir to the Dragon Throne, and he kept his own counsel. Would I ever be privy to it?

Thanourt grunted, staring into his own goblet. "No doubt, but if Shainakh marches on Pesh, prices will soar all about, and the Council is nervous."

"Yes. They are right to be." I took a long swallow of wine, wishing it was mead or even *hanta*. Getting drunk and picking Redfist's pocket had begun this mad chain of events, perhaps a good head-bending with liquor would end it. Thanourt gave me a strange look, and I roused myself to carry my end of the news-pole. It is how innkeeps and sellswords pay each other for annoyances, that balance. "They were announcing taxes on staples, searching for sellswords, and horseflesh was scarce between Hain and Vulfentown. Past that, I do not know. But yes, Pesh. Azkillian is a fool if he wishes another season in the grasslands; the Danhai are more demon than flesh."

"So I hear. I have also heard they kill a man, then bring him back to kill him again, slowly. Do they?"

"Never saw that." I took another gulp of wine. It didn't help. The screams, the grass, the blood, the yells of the tribesmen as they took scalps, or ears, or heads. Choking and coughing, retching the clear fluid of a lung-shot tinged with dark blood, Ammerdahl Rikyat had lain on my back like a breathing stone as I dragged him for the healers' tents. *You shall not die today. You owe me at dice.*

The Shainakh irregulars had begun to take trophies too, near the end of my stay. One half-Hain sellsword, Green-Eyes Ch'la, took to slipping out of camp at night and returning at dawn with blood-caked, flopping ears she pierced with bone needles and wore on a red string about her neck. For luck, she said.

She died in the same attack that nearly cost Rikyat his life. The Danhai had taken off her ears, fingers, nose, toes, and her breasts, before mounting her body on a pole. We found it during the next offensive, our cavalry riding deep into the Plains and overturning their empty camps. The Danhai had faded like ghosts, leaving only bodies and cold-char marks of tiny campfires.

Mud. Blood. Death.

"Kaia?" Darik touched my wrist. My hand lay flat upon the table, spread next to my bowl, tense as if it could dig past the cloth into the wood beneath. His fingertips were warm, and he tapped once, twice. "More wine?" Those fine manners, covering my lapse in attention, as if we were at a high table during a Festival dinner. Was I grateful?

"Yes." I should by all rights have lost my appetite thinking upon the wars on the grassplain sea, but a sellsword knows to eat when she can. Grief can wait; the belly needs its due even if the heart keens. "Shainakh has its gaze set on Pesh. I doubt they will succeed, but bleeding the young nobles and the military further may help keep the Emperor's grasp tight enough." Though even peasants may become restive, given enough hunger. A famine would wring Shainakh dry, and perhaps the Danhai would leave their grass and wreak vengeance upon the ancient bones of Azkillian's realm.

"Ai, but should he take Pesh, what next?" Thanourt shook his head, rubbing a blunt fingertip over the beads in his moustache. Worrying, the customary pastime of farmers and innkeeps alike.

"It might even be good for trade your trade, Nansouk's-kin. They will pay tribute until one of their own warlords gets restless. I have not passed that way in years, no doubt the players have changed. If Khma no Harvril is still the fire god's mouthpiece, they may even win a battle or two." *That* reed-straight, sword-rigid prince had defanged the temple priests *and* their wandering naked holy-talkers, and word had it some regarded him as a living flame kindled by their jealous, crackling god.

"Him? He died two summers ago. The mouthpiece is now one of the Chmi, a stripling brat who plays with poison. Good at it, too, to survive *that* nest of roasters." Thanourt did not rub at his wrists. He seemed to have forgotten the scars, and *that* was fine to see indeed.

"Hm." I settled in my chair, staring at my neglected bowl. Thanourt would report any lack of appetite to his husband, and a scolding from that mountain of a white-clad fishmonger was something I could do without. Still, my belly needed a moment to settle. "How far are their traders bringing new slaves from?"

"The usual places. No change there. The doors on the Street of Collars still abide." He did not turn ash-pale; that was good to see as well. Time had spread a healing upon him, more surely than any fleshstitcher or helpful witch.

Instead, *I* suppressed a shudder. There are no beggars on the Street of Collars. They learn early and well to stay away. "Then Pesh isn't expecting Azkillian to be serious. Perhaps they'll marry a princess off to buy an alliance, Azkillian has a few sons by his concubines. But Pesh...Chmi, hm? I don't know any of that clan, even by rumor." By the Moon, I never wished to visit Pesh again.

"Pious bastards, all the same." Thanourt spread his hands, his pinkish palms scarred with fine white well-healed lines. "Is the *chaabi* not good? Subo will be heartbroken."

I picked up my bowl. "The thought of Pesh curdles my appetite, Thanourt. But not for long."

"You have traveled that far?"

You should know, you met me not three days after I left. "The capital, once or twice. Slim pickings, no Guild there. All their thieves are freelance, and jealous of outlanders." I had been forced to assassination to gain enough coin to travel onward, and after two commissions had decided to leave. Pesh is strange, with its caged fires and naked holysingers with their long matted hair in the street, singing to their god of fire. All flame is sacred to them, meant to be held behind latticework or pierced metal. An unshielded candle, a campfire—those are somewhat blasphemous. The holysingers rave of their divine one's love and guidance, and in the next breath how all living creatures are his abject slaves.

"Ah. Yes." He waited for me to begin eating enough, his anxiety easing as I applied myself with flatbread and a long satisfying slurp. "Was your crossing hard?"

"We tangled with pirates—Scoryin, or at least they wore his flags. They had a windwitch, and the storm followed us. We sailed late."

"Indeed you did, the Night of Honey is two sevendays away."

I caught the subtle hint. "Before then we shall be settled in a villa uphill for the winter instead of keeping rooms you can charge double for during festivals, never fear."

"You are welcome to stay, Kaia-*luaha*." The honorific flowed easily from his tongue, a step up from the *hanua*. The latter was attached to a grown woman out of politeness, but the former is the closest thing Antai has to a noblewoman. "I have not forgotten what is owed." It was his turn to set his bowl aside, and I shook my head, my braids firmly in and the memories of that bloody afternoon so many years ago echoing. The sounds, the reek, the child's dark wide-open eyes, vacant with death, his swollen tongue protruding, and the slaver grunting atop the tiny body lashed to a timberhorse...

I had not gutted a man and left him before that day. I had thought denying a painless end not in my nature.

I found out differently in that instant. That particular slave-trader had *deserved* it, and what little guilt I felt for that murder was merely that I had waited a few moments before striking.

Did Ammerdahl Rikyat deserve his death too? The question clawed at me. In the heat of battle, it is in the hands of the gods—this one dies, this one lives, it is beyond an individual's power. Assassinations are slightly different, but still meant to be quick and relatively painless, and I chose my commissions with care. To be quick and ruthless is one thing.

The arrogance of meting out a slow painful end is another.

"No," I said, gently enough. "I would not burden you, Thanourt. I am glad to see you married, looking so fat and placid."

"We are not all meant for a life of excitement," he intoned, and hearing my own long-ago words from his mouth made a small, unwilling laugh rise, like a bubble under a ship's hull. It broke on my lips, and I did my best to soothe Thanourt and do justice to his husband's cooking at once. The rest of the news was interesting, but nothing in it touched upon any raw memory. Darik was silent all through the remainder of the meal, and afterwards asked only where I wished him to sleep.

Perhaps I should not have, but I pointed him to the bed. I took a blanket to the floor next to the fireplace. At least it was warm, and there were no rocks or ship-heaving underneath. He asked no questions, but then again, he would not need to.

Now we both knew I had left Ammerdahl Rikyat to die.

DUTIFUL

THE NEXT MORNING DAWNED CLEARER and cool, and
D'ri was awake before I surfaced from more restless
dreams. Consequently, who else would accompany me to
select a villa? Redfist was still snoring, Gavrin left at dawn
for some nebulous business, Diyan was too young, and
Janaire and Atyarik were behind their own closed door, no
doubt glad of the privacy. I could not leave a *s'tarei* behind
like a brace of saddlebags while I went marketing. Besides,
when dealing with land agents in Antai, tis best to bring
along a witness.

"Small," he said, examining the stone block topped
with tiles, its sharp defensible lines shouting its age—
before Antai ruled its own hinterlands, it was too valuable
to be left in peace by surrounding warlords. A clatter of
hooves and carter-cries splashed against the outer wall, but
the garden courtyard was quiet enough. "The roof is
sturdy, though."

"That is a blessing. Winter rains are harsh, here." For
once, I would be watching them from relative comfort
behind a window. It was a novel and extremely welcome
thought.

"As harsh as in Anjalismir?" He sounded merely
curious.

I did not flinch at the name of my childhood home. "Winter there is snow, not rain." Which he would know as well as I. Perhaps the silence wore on his nerves, as well.

"Does it snow here?"

It was a normal question from one who had not traveled to this corner of the world before. Why, then, did I sense trouble looming, like the Shelt's storms waiting to sweep inland? "Not so much, close to the sea. They say that under the Pensari sometimes the bay froze, but others disagree. Do you prefer this one?"

"The house? The other, with the practice-ground...though I liked not its foundations, they were freshly plastered."

"So you noticed. Sharp eyes, on my *s'tarei*."

Could I call him that, without a pinch of guilt just under my breastbone? I was not what is prized in *adai*, I could not forget as much even for a moment. Though Darik's expression relaxed slightly, as he studied the roof beams. The agent was taking his ease in a hired *dabui* outside, probably wishing we would invite him to a luncheon. In return he might suddenly remember a jewel of property instead of the ones he had shown us so far.

Business takes time, the proverb ran. Or, *a rich man takes a long season to move his bowels*. They mean the same thing.

I was just about to congratulate myself on setting my princeling at ease when he dropped his chin and gave me a sharp, level look, his mouth a thin line and his dark eyes afire.

"I would ask you a question, *adai'mi*."

So I was right. Trouble. I told myself it could very well be a simple, commonplace bit of business. More inquiries about the city, about the inn, about this patch of the Rim. "Yes?"

"Was he your lover?" He used the most polite term tradetongue had for a whore's patron, but the G'mai words around it gave the context. There is no word for *adultery* in

G'mai, or for a lover who is not your twin. There is little need.

What? "Who?"

"Your Rikyat." His lip did not curl, but I suspect it was only through sheer force of will. He still did not look at me, instead studying the view of Antai's lower hills, visible over the top of a stone wall trailed with ambitious vines—they looked decorative instead of useful, the broad leaves turning crimson and gold with the advent of harvest. It looked related to Thasonni grapevines, but without the distinctive pink threading through the leaves and stems. I could identify edible and medicinal; the ornamentals were of no use. The Shainakh goddess of grain and grape, slaughter and fermenting, would frown on such a thing as a useless plant in a garden. Which was no worry of mine, since the Moon is jealous of her children and keeps them from the influence of other gods.

That same harvest-goddess had been behind Rikyat, they said.

I cleared my throat, suppressing an urge to spit as if he was a fellow sellsword prying at me. "No. I owed him a debt, tis all."

A muscle in Darik's cheek flickered. "What of the barbarian? Was he?"

The sense of the world slipping away underneath me returned, as if the Lan'ai had not yet loosed its grasp upon my legs. A *s'tarei* did not speak so. The word for *jealousy* in our language cannot be applied to people, only to possessions and some few intangibles—political power, perhaps a talent. I might have laughed, if my hands had not tensed, wanting to curl into fists. My anger, or his? "I hardly had time. And again, I owed him a debt, having picked his pocket and caused him some trouble." My throat was dry. I fixed my gaze to the same point he seemed to be staring at, a particular crimson leaf large enough to hide a hand. Perhaps it was a grapevine after all, though it bore no fruit this year.

A muscle flicked once on his shaven cheek. *S'tarei* do not wear beards. "Am I a debt? Do you feel you *owe*?"

How could I answer that? A *s'tarei* is a gift from the Moon, just as an *adai* is. "More than I can repay." My stomach had turned to a knot, as if I were facing my first pitched battle, again. Except there was no dust, no mud, no screaming of horse or sellsword, no reek of cut bowel or iron tang of blood. Merely a neglected ruin of a once-pretty garden. Weeds poked through gravel and crowded the flagstones, and though the roof was sturdy one or two of the rooms were much damper than I liked.

No. This place would not do at all, especially if I had to daily pass over a patch of earth that had held this conversation.

"D'ri..." How on earth could I explain? "You must understand. For *years* I was the only G'mai who walked alone. I knew I was flawed. Such knowledge leaves a mark."

He shook his head slightly, and even with that mutinous glow to his eyes and line to his chin, he could have been a statue—had the Folk been in the habit of making them for the arrogance of our ruling family. In Shaituh, images of Azkillian's portly scowl were everywhere. There were even temples built to the God-Emperor, a colonnade of marbles bearing the likeness of each crowned despot.

"What I understand," he answered, "is that I should have left earlier. But I was *dutiful*. I did what was required of me, and it almost cost my *adai*."

At least now I knew he *had* a temper. It was more comforting than it should have been, to push him into such irritation. "That is past. It does no good to—"

"Are you shamed by your *s'tarei*? I was *obedient*, instead of seeking you. Perhaps I should have matched your stubbornness with my own."

"You are doing as much at this very moment," I muttered. It was not helpful, and neither was the complex, bubbling heat welling up inside me. Had it been a fellow sellsword, I would have been walking away or reaching for my *dotani*. "Mother Moon, what do you *want* of me?"

"Nothing I may have, apparently."

A nest of swallows under the roof woke, and wingbeats pulsed elsewhere as well. City-noise—carts rumbling, animals lowing or shrieking, voices raised or low—filled the short painful quiet. I turned, my bootheel stabbing a yellowflower weed, and stalked for the entrance. This house was not large enough, and come the rainy season we might be standing in water instead of it dripping upon us from an ill-patched roof.

"Kaia." He did not say it very loudly, and I pretended not to hear, my teeth aching as my jaw bore down.

There were still three villas to view, but I paid the agent copper for his time and sent him away. The long trek back to the inn, with Darik's presence at my shoulder, was twice as uncomfortable as setting out had been. He said my name once more, but I did not respond.

If I had, I might have said something unforgivable.

Until You Know

THE QUIETEST CORNER OF THE commonroom was awash with gasping, but it was merry instead of pained. Redfist spread his hands, his blue eyes twinkling above his beard— now oiled, and beaded as they do in Antai, with bright blue clay beads. "And there I was," he said, while Janaire laughed helplessly, jewel-bright tear tracks on her soft cheeks. Diyan giggled next to me, his small body quivering with amusement, and even Atyarik was smiling ruefully. "Holding a cow's arsehole closed so the guts wouldna spill, while my father and Uncle Dorak rolled on the floor, mucked up with blood and everything else, and at that very moment me mam arrives." His voice lifted slightly, into a lilting caricature of a woman's. "*And what is all this now?*"

Darik snorted, a short sharp sound of repressed merriment. Gavrin, licking grease from lamb *couria* off his fingers, almost choked on a mouthful of flatbread and pushed his chair back, tossing his hair with a quick habitual flick. He was trying to eat and tune his lute at the same time, and almost injuring himself with either in turn.

"So, me mam leans down," Redfist continued, and I caught myself in a hiccoughing laugh, sharp wine burning in my throat and up into the back of my nose. "And she grabs *both* of them by the hair, and knocks their heads together, like *so!*" He slammed his fists enthusiastically against each other, thumping the bottom of the table with his knee for good measure. I tilted my head back to force some of the wine out of my nose and back into my throat. Irrigating one's head with Antai red is a painful experience. "So now I am holding a cow's arsehole, Uncle Dorak is cursing, my father bites Dorak's hand, and my mother is crying at both of them to stop acting like bairns." He took a deep breath. "And then...I couldna help myself."

Another pause. He raised his tankard and took a pull of ale. The table held several denuded dishes, and several ears in other areas of the commonroom were listening now. The tall red one had a knack for telling stories.

"No, I couldna help myself," Redfist said, slowly, spreading the fingers of his free hand to illustrate. "I *let go*."

A roar of laughter, table-pounding, and groans echoed through the commonroom. I pitched sideways, my belly aching from the merriment, and fetched up against D'ri's shoulder. He didn't seem to mind, bent over slightly with his head down as he shook. Janaire's tears gleamed afresh, and she held her sides; Atyarik uttered a short bark of amusement. Diyan almost slid under the table, and Gavrin choked again, his fingers stuttering on the strings and producing a squawk that only added to the hilarity.

The great swell of noise retreated, but Redfist had his flagon held high, as if signaling for more ale. "I learned a philosophic lesson then, my friends, and I learned it well."

"What lesson?" someone called across the commonroom.

Redfist's grin could not be wider, his teeth flashing through his beard and his flagon quivering slightly. "Never, *ever*, let go of an arsehole, *until* you know he willna spray you!"

The entire commonroom exploded with laughter. Fresh drinks were called for—Thanourt would be happy of the extra custom. Now Gavrin, licking his fingers afresh, settled a little closer to the fire and began to play, softly at first, running up and down hills of notes to test the lute's voice. Redfist downed another hefty swallow of ale and let out a mannerly belch.

Mannerly by his standards, at least, since it did not rattle every bit of crockery in the room.

Darik leaned close, his lips at my ear, warm breath touching my cheek. "I am sorry," he murmured, in G'mai. The inflection—*s'tarei* to *adai*, quiet and intimate—and his breath sent a scalding through me. "I should not have said such things."

No. You should not have. But my own tone was just as hesitant. "Forgiven, Dragaemir Darikaan. Think no more upon it." Very formal, but I used the answering inflection to his—the weight on the first syllable and the lilt at the end we call *ad'aila*, the lover's tongue. The songs written for such speech are not sung at gatherings or festivals, only given voice in small private settings.

I had never thought I would speak to another in such a way. Gavrin struck the strings in a fan of melody, a rolling sea-rhythm of what had to be a new song.

"I do." D'ri ignored the sound. "You were not the only one walking alone."

It was like a shallow slice from a fresh-whetted blade, so sharp the blood does not begin to flow for some moments, as if the body does not comprehend its injury. I dropped my gaze to my plate, my eating-picks set neatly to the side of its wooden face, and a cracked fowl-bone I had stripped the marrow from with relish. A sellsword's habit, to consume everything that could be eaten. Some even gnaw the bones, believing it makes their teeth stronger.

Gavrin's large hands, too big for the rest of him, plucked and strummed and beat, and when the crowd had quieted enough, he began to sing.

"*Oh, the Steelflower took ship a-to the Lan'ai, With an elvish prince and a little boy, A man of red and a witch besides, And a*

long-faced elvish monk in stride, hey ho, hey la, we've all gone to sea—
"

I pushed my chair back, rising swiftly. The commonroom went back to its regular surf-roar. Another Iron Flower song, they had heard them all. He would have better luck with a story of Kruk the Merciless or a lay of the Khana Alhari, or even a simple drinking song. Other sellswords had proper minstrels, I was saddled with a Pesh lutebanger with less sense than a sack of wet rocks. Not enough sense to stay belowdecks during a battle, even, and I perhaps owed him Darik's life.

A heavy debt, as the G'mai counted things. So I made for the stairs, and when D'ri fell into step behind me, I did not look back. The Night of Honey was approaching, I needed to find a suitable villa—and a better agent to purchase one, since the first had been a dismal piece of greased soap. Thanourt was abashed—he had sent me to that office without realizing his favored agent had moved to the Street of Blue Cloth.

Head down, I navigated the stairs, reached my own door, and half-turned as if to bid D'ri a good night.

His expression stopped me. Had his gaze been fixed on my nape the entire way? Now it fastened on my mouth. His hair had shaken loose from laughter, and it suited him very much. He stepped forward, crossing the invisible border between *me* and the outside world, and I might have stepped back, but the door was there.

I froze. Like a rabbit under a hawk's claws, or a sellsword in her first brush with violence, immobilized until the body begins to move as it has been trained to. The rabbit dies, the sellsword—if she is lucky, and has not shirked her practice—may live to fight another battle, and have only scarring to show for it.

It is the blood rising, Kaia. That is all. The twin-bond is intensely physical, too. Neither of us had a choice, I told myself, even as a thin thread of baffled anger lit inside me.

I was no Gullah holy-singer, barred from fleshly pleasures—but I was no Rijiin courtesan either. Oh, it is not unknown for two *adai* to be...close, and sometimes two *s'tarei* as well. Affection is never to be wasted.

And yet.

Nose to nose, we stared at each other. His beautiful eyes, iris and pupil blending, the faint wrinkles at the corners shouting he was well past the age we are normally *twinned* at. I sipped at his breath, *coura* spices and the wine's fruity exhalation mingling between us.

"What do you see?" I whispered.

I could even feel his lips move. Was he closer? "My *adai.*" Silent words bloomed, tentatively, in the voice-within's warmth. *What else is there?*

Still, I hesitated. I was not fine enough for him, and well I knew it.

You were not the only one who walked alone. However cruel my own flaws were, how much worse could it have been for a *s'tarei*, trammeled as he was by the Queen and perhaps...perhaps he had worried that his twin would take ill and die, if he lingered. It is the terror of a *s'tarei*, to allow injury to his twin.

I felt for the doorlatch at my hip, lifted it. The knob turned easily, and Darik straightened. A flash of hurt sparked, deep in those so-dark eyes, and I gathered myself.

"Come in." My mouth had gone dry and the wine-fumes ignited in my head. "*S'tarei'mi.*"

It was only the blood-heat. He had told me he would not touch me until I wished it, and I was not sure I did. But I did not say *no*, and I thought I could well endure it, if it would make him...happy.

A LONG AFTERNOON

DARIK TURNED ASIDE TO EXAMINE a knife-seller's wares, so Redfist and I cast about for a place to wait. Even in Antai, the presence of a Skaialan giant gives one some elbow-room in a market crowd. I juggled the paper-wrapped pasty from hand to hand, waiting for it to cool. "You are a piece of luck, my friend."

Redfist did the same with his own greasy-wrapped bundle of meat and flaky golden crust, the same boyish, wide, white smile splitting his beard. "Thought you would never admit it, lass."

My answering grin, for once, did not feel strange or strained at all. I caught sight of a tiny flickering motion and warned the pickpocket—a Pesh with hair the color of dirty straw and a red-striped jerkin—away with a small answering motion of my own. She faded aside into the crowd. I wished her good pickings, just not from *my* purse. In great cities, the thieves are more determined, and later in winter they might be harder to dissuade. After the Sunreturn it's best not to venture into certain alleys alone, even if you have faith in your steel and your wits.

None of that mattered at the moment, for the sun was bright and a cool breeze carried the stink across the bay into the Lan'ai's throat, replacing the steam-reek with mountain-fragrance and tinges of smoke that said *harvest, festival, plenty.* To judge by the merriness in the Ketle-jua Market, there was no drought in Antai's hinterlands. Already the farmers had come forth, their waggons loaded high with first fruits they would sell for a handsome profit, keeping the bulk of their ripening crops for later in the season when the cold began to bite. Every lutebanger at every corner or jammed between stalls was singing a threshing-song, or a scything-chants, accompanied by pipe or stringed instruments of every description. Stone and timber buildings crowded each other as well, taverns with doors thrown open and inns with criers shouting the number of rooms and the start-bargain price, outdoing each other to bring in the weary or sullen. The stall owners, mostly round women with kerchiefs, most with the wide copper faces of Antai's melding-pot and the chestnut tinge to their dark hair that bespoke some diluted Pensari ancestry, sang their wares too.

The din was titanic, horrifying, and marvelous. There is a solace in that noise, especially if one has received a little training to keep the borders of body and mind inviolate. With the *taih'adai*'s help, I no longer felt buffeted by waves of confusion from every quarter. I had never thought much of it—there is a word in every tongue for those who dislike crowds—because I thought I had no Power, so my distaste for large gatherings was normal. When you do not know the alternative, almost any feature of a life can seem inevitable. Gods-decreed, even.

Even the acrobats dancing through the crowd, whisking around a basket for copper bits, did not trouble me as they used to.

Plenty of reasons to feel merry, not the least of which was our ruddy barbarian's size making negotiating for the villa we would winter in *much* easier. He knew a fair bit about leases, too, which surprised me—he asked one or two questions about terms and agreements that magically reduced the price by increments, which left more of the redgold Shainakh Rams with their mellow shine for winter's food and clothing. In spring I would have to make decisions, but between Redfist's pointed questions and Darik's air of nobility, we had secured much better quarters than I thought likely. Janaire was supervising the move of our luggage, having shooed us away for the afternoon. *You'll only be underfoot. Leave me the boy and my s'tarei, 'tis all, and stay out of trouble.* A hen too young to mother, pecking and practicing.

I shook away the nipping worry of next year's food and shelter, watched a knot of Kmeri plainsdwellers come to trade horses and leather. They gawped openly at the sights, and their high-crested hair gave me a faint unease.

The Danhai wear their hair shaved at the sides and crested at the top as well, greasing it into stiffness and tying colored thread into the tufts to denote clan, family, and other allegiances. The Kmeri prize blue for their skygod, and streak clay dyed with a noisome root that produces a bright, bold cobalt through their hair. The shadow of a crested head at the edge of sight can send your hand twitching for a blade, if you have survived even a few days of that bloody morass the Shainakh emperor was so set on grinding through.

We set our backs to a patch of sun-warmed wall and ate our meatpies with goodwill and almost-burned tongues. I restrained the urge to lick greasy paper, a remnant of hungrier times. Redfist had finished his before I was half done, and I sensed he might have a dry throat afterward. D'ri leaned closer to the knife-seller, listening intently, and if I focused, I could probably *hear* what the merchant was saying to my *s'tarei*.

I did not, glancing instead at Redfist. He gazed over the market with obvious delight, and I was hard-put to suppress another smile.

When he glanced down at me, blue eyes twinkling, his expression changed a bit. "So. Trouble with your Darrak, then?" His broad accent flattened the first syllable of the name, instead of caressing the *a*, and further turned the middle consonant into a harsh burr.

Not precisely. We had accorded each other the very strictest of courtesy since he had awakened to find me already dressed and intending to leave the inn. I shrugged, folding the paper several times. They make it from rice, like the Hain, and during some famines the poor would chew it into a sludge, hoping for some nutriment. Even in good times ragpickers collected these shreds; bales of them were turned into fresh paper, but no doubt more than a few ended in a hungry belly. "When is there not?"

"Ye've a sharp mind, and a tongue to match. Ye may find *he* does as well."

Thank you, my giant red friend. How would I think of such things without you to say them aloud? "There are complexities, Redfist. And..." The words trembled in the back of my throat. He had been with Diyan, Gavrin, and the other G'mai during the battle, he only knew what D'ri had told them. They had called me *honorable*.

Were they fools, or was I? All of us, perhaps.

"And?" A gentle prodding. I would not have expected it from a burly, flour-skinned barbarian nearly thrice my size with blunt sausage-fingers.

"*My luck will turn against me*, Rikyat said." I squeezed the paper, my knuckles turning white. "And it did. I left him to die."

"Was he your *cor'jhan* too, then?" Redfist's brow furrowed.

It had taken some time before I thought I understood just what that Skaialan word meant, but when I did, it was no surprise. Men were always knotting the same string, the one stuffed in their trews. "I am not a courtesan, Redfist. He was my friend."

"Seems a funny bit of friendship, to try to kill ye. Not once but twice."

"Thrice if you count the battle." It came sharper than I meant it, but something tight-wound in me eased. He had a point.

"Once would be more than enough, lass. Ye feel a *duthnning*, then?"

"A doo-vrong?" I could not fit my mouth around the word. At that time, I did not know much Skaialan, and there is a trick to that language. More than one, indeed.

"*Duthnning*. A debt repaid but still...there." He spread his hands. "We have words for it, trade-talk doesnae satisfy."

"Indeed it does not. There are terms in G'mai that—"

I might have said more, but a shadow fell over me, and I had my hand on a knifehilt before Redfist gave a pleased grunt, straightening from the wall and pushing past me. "As I live and breathe! Corran!"

It was another Skaialan giant, this one not so ruddy but Clau-fair instead, with only a tinge of russet to his beard. The rest of him was so filthy it was difficult to tell much more. He lacked a half-head of Redfist's height, but his shoulders were just as wide, and he was just as white-skinned and full-bearded. He smelled ripe as a fish barrel left in the sun for three days, and his eyes were a much paler blue. Along the Lanai Shairukh coast such a color might be a held in caution, just as my own golden gaze had been.

"*Rainak!*" the new arrival bellowed, and they threw their arms about each other, Redfist pounding the man on the back and being threshed in return. I watched this, my head tilted in wonderment, and finally their greetings subsided to a low rumble instead of thunder. Darik, catching wind of the commotion, glanced up, and began making his way through the crowd.

"Kaia!" Redfist outright *beamed*, his fine large teeth peeking through his beard. "Tis Corran Ninefinger, of the

Riverled Gannot! Corran, ye bastard, meet the finest sellsword in this part of the world, Kaahai Ironflower!"

I would have bowed, but was instead enveloped in a rib-cracking, reeking embrace. "Proud to meet ye, lass!" Corran boomed, and I was beginning to feel a little faint by the time he turned me loose. Darik arrived just in time, and I laid a hand on his arm with a meaningful look.

A *s'tarei* does not allow another to touch his *adai,* unless she wishes it. This new giant was foul, but he meant no harm.

Or at least, I did not *think* he did. Not then.

"Be careful," Redfist bellowed. "She picks pockets, she does! Come, come, we need ale!"

Dear gods. I was the one with the coin, so, dragged along in their wake, D'ri and I followed the two giants through the Market and into a close, dark, overly warm hole of a tavern, where a round of dry sweet Hinterland hop-brew began what promised to be a very long afternoon.

A FINE DISTINCTION

I WOKE WITH A POUNDING head, my *dotani* clearing the sheath with its familiar whisper. For a moment I was back in Hain, too much mead the night before and the Guards approaching with the hush that meant bloodshed dogged their steps. Steel sparked, honed edges sliding, and I went over backward, kicking the table leg to drive the entire wooden edifice into my opponent. Gained my feet with a lurch, and heard hurried, stealthy movement. Bars of dust-laden sunlight pierced the shutters, mornlight robbed of its vigor by the gloom in the corners.

He moved to my left, gracefully avoiding the table, and I halted my lunge just in time. Darik, however, slapped my blade aside with his right-hand *dotani* as if he expected me not to halt, and I sank back on my heel, bracing myself for the next move, which would be his own thrust.

My head pounded, I probably had ale in my braids, and my mouth tasted like the bottom of a byre the stable-boys are too busy to clean in summer.

I straightened, retreating another step to take me from the semicircle of his range.

His face hardened slightly—of course, no true *adai* would greet morning in a tavern still soused from the night before. There was a hazy memory of Redfist challenging me cup for cup, and him and his friend Corran sliding under the table while I triumphantly finished a measure of *hanta*.

Mother Moon, had I really called for *hanta*? I winced at the thought. The colorless, fiery Shainakh liquor could poison you if not treated with a modicum of respect.

I suspected I had been less than careful *or* respectful last night. Where had Darik been? I had lost track after the second round of the mead-battle. I did remember his dark gaze, at various points, but it had not seemed very important.

D'ri's *dotanii* flashed, ending their complicated spin secured to his back. He straightened too, combat-stance fading. I finally glanced about. A few shapeless lumps face down on tables; it was no doubt very early. No sign of the giant and his friend.

I could believe my life had slipped back into its well-worn ruts, if not for the Dragaemir princeling standing, straight and iron-faced, looking not quite at me but at some point past my shoulder. My *dotani* slid back into its sheath, with a rasping whisper. My hands were perhaps not quite steady.

Finally, he broke the silence, in pure lilting G'mai. "The large red one returned to the inn with his new friend. You seemed disposed to stay."

My head gave a heatless twinge of pain. It served me right, drinking the afternoon with giants is all but guaranteed to end badly. My own words came with only a hint of slur. "I have not been this drunk since Hain." Tradetongue, its hills and valleys suddenly betraying me, because through them, like rocks thrusting through topsoil, were the cadences of my birthtongue.

Darik took a step forward, I retreated once more, a light shuffling move learned in many a tavern brawl. It was instinctive, but perhaps it gave the wrong impression.

His expression darkened further. "Have I given you any reason to fear me?" His hands tensed, I sensed them wanting to curl onto themselves, knuckles wanting to whiten. "Any at *all*?"

I almost winced yet again. Did he think bedplay had turned me into a fleeing maiden, like the Clau tales of girls shapeshifting to trees to escape amorous deities? I was no maid, and he was no god. "I do not fear you." There, in the accent of my youth, the thorny pleasure of speaking G'mai. You may learn a thousand tongues, but the one you are born to is always there, an underground river. "I fear..."

What? What is it Kaia Steelflower, the Iron Flower they sing cheap ditties about in taverns, worth good red gold to any who want a sword's service—what is it you fear?

He waited. No doubt I was straining his patience. I did nothing *but* strain the patience of any I allowed too close to me, any I...

I finally gathered enough spit in my dry, dry mouth to shape the next words. "No doubt you saw much to anger you last night."

Darik regarded me quietly, top to toe, from my scarred boots to my mussed braids, my indifferently-mended jerkin and my harsh trews, the dirt on my face and the rancid breath of inebriation filling my throat.

"When the moment comes that I am *angered*," he said, clearly, "I will not hesitate to inform you. I was pleased to accompany you. You might have been stabbed or worse, were you alone and unaware."

A *s'tarei* is responsible for an *adai*'s protection, ever and always. Power moves in the women of the G'mai, and to teach us the meaning of mercy we feel any harm committed to our twin's flesh. The balance is there, between the not-so-visible Power and the all too visible responsibility. Most know not to attempt any mischief on a drunken sellsword's person, only their purse, but what if I had attracted more notice than was wise? He fought well, but a tavern knifebrawl was an unpredictable battleground at best, and I had placed him in danger.

Again.

Janaire had the right of it. Had I stayed home, in G'maihallan...

But I had not, and that was past, and what I had at the moment was a tavern full of creaking drunks who were beginning to stir, and the knowledge that my purse was several coins lighter. Money to get us through the winter, and I had squandered some portion of it. Just like any common sellsword. Not to mention a *s'tarei* I had not spoken more than courtesies to after our first blood-encounter. He was somewhat inexperienced, true, but not...not precisely *bad*, and feeling his half of the play had some very interesting effects.

Was I blushing? "I do not fear you." Once I said it, my throat eased slightly. "You must believe that."

"Then I will." Darik took another step. I did not retreat, though I twitched. He simply offered his hand, palm-up. Said nothing. In Vulfentown there had been the twinsickness; I could not tell myself it had merely been a *jai* fever, prone to recurrence once you had suffered it. I could not tell myself much of anything at all. I longed for a bath, for a flesh-kneader at the temple, and for another few kegs of *hanta* to lose myself in.

Rikyat and I had matched each other with *hanta* in his army camp, the night before the battle. A thimbleful before a pitched battle is the custom, but in the irregulars, it pays to be generous.

My calluses scraped against Darik's palm. Another reminder of what I was, and what I would never be—a soft G'mai girl, the *adai* he had been cheated of.

"I suspect you craved refuge in forgetting, for a short while." He folded both his hands over mine. "Him. Ammerdahl." Very softly, his accent turning the name into an exotic featherbrush. "His rebellion failed."

There was nothing I wanted more than some fresh *hanta* to drown the sound of my own thoughts repeated to me in clear, tender G'mai, the most intimate of inflections. My mouth was so foul I could not bear to breathe upon him. That was the reason I dropped my chin, perhaps. For the moment, the black silk over his chest seemed the least troubling alternative. "He said I was his luck. And luck would desert him, if I..."

"Ah. Was that what he cried as you left?"

Of course, the Shainakh would not be so clear to my *s'tarei*, in the post-battle din. "Yes." My eyes burned. There was no weeping in me, I told myself. I almost added the dream, but that would raise another specter—more lessons with Janaire, and the *fatahn'adai*, the future-knowing, was nothing to be wished for. Besides, it wasn't precisely future-knowing if it showed the past, was it? It was only a *dream*; I had a full waggonload of problems. Adding one more would be folly.

His shoulders slackened. *"Shaurauq'g'd'ia,"* he breathed. It is one of the stronger imprecations a *s'tarei* may utter. "May he be cursed."

"Cursed or not, his luck abandoned him." When you have fought side by side with a man, when he has taken a crossbow bolt for you, when you have dragged him to the healer's tents and fought off Danhai raiders on horseback, when you kept watch at his side after the tribesfolk had been beaten away and chewed flavourless dried horsemeat with the salt stinging your mouth while he shudders and fights to breathe...even if that man seeks to use you afterward, even if he set a Blue Hand at you and would have gladly sacrificed you in the front of a battle because his god told him so...

Even then, what you hear is the sound of a crossbow, the bolt splitting air, the knowledge that you cannot move in time, and a shadow between you and death grunts and falls. Your own place in the Halls of the Moon is taken. I found myself leaning forward, perhaps because the world had not finished its shifting underneath me.

D'ri was right, I had sent Redfist and his friend home and continued to well and truly sot myself, in the time-honored fashion of sellswords, to salve an ache there was no cure for.

If Thanourt could lay aside the coverings for the marks on his wrists, perhaps after some measure of seasons I could think on Ammerdahl Rikyat without the sharp pinch of...what? Grief? Of all the languages I could handle, there did not seem to be a word that applied.

Even in G'mai.

My forehead met Darik's chest. He was still as a stone, the faint rise of his breathing halting for a moment. Then he inhaled, and his voice was a comforting rumble. "He sent a *skai'atair* to kill his luck." The word holds many meanings—unclean, foul, outcaste, the dregs of a poisoned bowl. *Assassin*, as well. "Is that the custom, in these strange lands?"

At least I had the benefit of *understanding* Antai, Vulfentown, Shainakh. Darik, fresh from G'maihallan, Janaire and Atyarik had all traveled, certainly, but mine was the sellsword's way. You learn quickly, or you die, and I had gained my understanding with both time and blood.

My shoulders dropped still further. I leaned into him as if I were a ship, and he a safe harbor. He still held my fingers, but touched one of my sadly abused braids, a gentle, skating motion, as well.

"Not the custom." I said into his shirt, wishing my head would cease pounding. "More the rule."

"A fine distinction, *adai'mi*." Quiet, gentle, as if I were a horse to be soothed.

The thought of a *s'tarei* to a horse made my breath hitch in, then out in short chuffing gasps. Darik's arms closed about me, and I did not know whether I was weeping or laughing onto his fine silk and leather. In the middle of a just-rousing Antai tavern, the clenching in my chest loosened a little, then a little more. When he drew me out into the too-bright streets of the mist-locked city, I followed, my hand caught in his as if I trusted him, and my head empty of all but a great ringing unsound.

BAFFLE AND
BREECHES

BREATHING, IN AND OUT, a comforting rhythm. Complete darkness, for my arm was over my eyes, sealing out the faint glow of the banked fire. Darik's inhalations were long and quiet, his exhalations the same. It was...pleasant, his arm across my belly and his mouth near my bare shoulder. Every so often his hand might twitch or his dark lashes flutter, not signs of restlessness but of deep dreaming.

I tried to match his breath with my own. I listened to the creaks and groans—any house, especially an Antai stone-and-timber villa midway up the hills, sings at night. The kitchen was stocked enough for a tenday, Janaire had taken over the cooking with a sigh of relief, declaring inn-fare passable but nothing more; our first meal in our new home had been merry enough. She made *skanta*, and made it well, despite some of G'maihallan's spices missing. They did not travel even so far as Hain, the flavours of my homeland.Gavrin attempted to strike up his song about the crossing again and was hissed at, Diyan had a long face because he had his own room—he'd grown quite used to sleeping next to Redfist, but I did not trust this Ninefinger enough to let a child rest near him. Still, the boy badgered

Gavrin into playing some freetown drinking-songs, and that lightened the mood considerably.

Ninefinger himself was not so hearty an eater as Redfist, but he did not look askance at a free meal. It worried me, slightly. I did not like the idea of two giants to feed, and somehow the conversation had never turned to what business, precisely, the blond barbarian was in Antai upon.

D'ri moved slightly, his arm brushing my hip. Sleeplessness had left its mark on him. Perhaps he was not quite as used to it as I had become. Or perhaps my sotted stupor the previous night had given me a surfeit of rest.

The little Vulfentown boy would need proper winter trews and jerkin, and would likely outgrow both by spring. Now that we were settled for this season, I could begin to plan for the next. I could not drag the entire troupe about for the rest of my life, could I? Janaire and Atyarik could return to G'maihallan whenever they pleased, what kept them was my unfinished training and perhaps their fealty to Darik. At least *he* was not subtly hinting at homesickness. Redfist could sellsword with me; it could even be an advantage. The boy, though...did I really think him fit for a thief's life? He was quick and capable, and most thieves are winnowed early; he was past the most dangerous age.

Gavrin was all but useless, especially if I wished to hie myself to any city I required a decent amount of anonymity in.

A sharp dissatisfied sigh caught me unaware, but Darik's breathing didn't alter. It was useless. I would not sleep that night, between the worry and—useless to deny it—the dread of another dream. Battles sometimes returned while a sellsword visited the night country, often bleeding into what *could* have happened instead of what *had*. There was no reason to suspect anything more, but such apprehension is not a philosopher to be argued with. All that soothes it is time.

I finally slid carefully from under D'ri's arm. It was a chance to practice silent-moving, a thieves' skill indeed. The trick is to spread your weight slowly against the floorboards, and to count—and remember—your steps in *any* house. Ghosting across the room, barefoot, standing in the hall to wriggle into my breeches and shrug into my unlaced shirt once the door was safely closed, I immediately felt much better.

Careful, precise prowling is a brand of moving, and motion helps thinking. There were no guards posted and I was not here to relieve a treasury of its cargo, and the unfamiliar sounds of the house would mask my stealthy creeping. Down the stairs, testing my memory of their squeaks and dimensions, wringing a betraying whisper out of one and chastising myself sharply for it. On the lower floor, stone underfoot chill-hard, wind mouthing the corners of the house, I paused to fix the stairs more clearly in my memory. Going *up* would be different, and I did not wish to make a sound upon my return. I should have felt better, but irritation settled just under my roughening skin.

I turned towards the kitchens. I had bought a double-fistful of *kafi* beads, now might be a good time to grind and brew some, sip at something hot while the night breathed around me. It was not raining, and in the shelter of the courtyard it would be warm enough, even barefoot, as long as I kept moving.

I closed my eyes, running my fingertips lightly over the wall on my right. One, two, three openings—a shuttered window, another, then the door leading to the tiled room with two bathing-tubs. We could even hire a servant or two, and without the drudgery of cleaning or cooking I could perhaps study something. Poetry, or history; there were no shortage of scrollsters on the Street of Dust and its branching capillaries.

Wait.

The door moved slightly under my fingers. Everything inside me tightened.

It was open; the latch was not caught. I replayed the evening in my head. Diyan had taken the office of closing and latching, just as a pot-boy in an inn might. It was unlike him to perform slipshod any task I gave him.

I lifted the latch bar, and it moved smoothly. My nostrils flared slightly—a distinctive odor.

Cras oil.

My free hand flashed to my hip, but no knifehilt greeted me. It could simply be our little thief-boy, taking it upon himself to quiet a squeak or two—except he had barely been able to stay awake at the end of dinner, stuffed to the backteeth with Janaire's *skanta.*

My skin crawled, little skittering feet of unease prowling every inch of me. *Stop. Think.*

If I were about quiet business, I might have tested the kitchen's back door, easily propped open to allow a breeze through when the ovens drew out cooksweat. There was a short passage to the *prasium*—the room where lather from *cras*-oil soap would be scraped from a rich Antai merchant's skin before he plunged into a bath tepid or scalding—that a servant could take to bring the fruits it was customary to sample while bathing from downcellar or kitchen cupboard. This was a small villa, without a grand dining room or the *scilbahua*, the bathing-room that could seat enough of the city's powerful to sit in steam and decide matters of policy or trade.

The mental walls between me and the outer world thinned, an instinctive reaching-out. I had shifted my weight back, intending to slide up the stairs and at least fetch a knife, when a small deadly hiss, lost under the sound of the wind, slid past my ear.

When a knifeblade is traveling quickly enough, it cleaves air and pushes a deathbreeze before it.

I was already moving, pitching aside and ducking, my left foot flicking back to catch a knee. A faint brush of cloth against my toes and I went down all the way, shock of stone flooring unsweetened by carpet or rushes against my knee, tucking and rolling to take myself out of range. My pupils dilated, the shadow moved, and a flickering gleam told me *curved blade, can't blacken the honed edge itself* as I gained my feet with a silent lunge. As tall as me, slightly broader at shoulder and narrower at hip, the intruder kicked, meaning to throw me off balance, but I was already leaning back and shuffling, toes spread to grip and everything but the knife-edge vanishing from my consciousness. *Could have another blade...move, move move!*

Another low deadly note, and *that* answered me. Two knives, and all I had was the shirt I was tearing at and my wits. "*Hai!*" I yelled, and flung myself aside again. We had exchanged places now, my back to the stairs and the intruder hesitating just out of range.

Thief, or assassin? The next moment or two would give me an answer.

The shape darted for me, I threw myself back again, finally tearing the cloth and laces of my shirt enough to free it from my shoulders and arms, wrapping it over my left arm as a baffle as I gave yet more ground, retreating for the stairwell's foot. Another lunge, the cloth on my arm was thin protection and if I took a strike there was the best place. To coldly calculate catching a knife in your own arm-muscle is no pleasant task.

True combat brings out the water, even in one or two passes. Tiny puffs of chill over my sweating skin, my breasts bounced slightly as I dodged yet another strike, and if the assassin was fast enough they could cut off the stairs and work me toward the kitchen. At least there were blades there, unless Janaire had locked the cupboard.

Edged metal caught cloth, tearing, sharp tip caressing the back of my forearm, a lick of fire and first blood to this shadow. I dropped as if something vital had been hit or I had tripped, both legs flung out as the stone burned my bare back, and just caught one dark-wrapped knee. Not enough to injure, but it threw the intruder's pattern off, and I rolled, knowing if I could just move, just *move*, I could gain my feet and there was a spindly table from previous inhabitants on this side of the hall, ugly enough to be left behind. It was better than nothing, once I had one of its legs within range I would be armed, after a fashion, and—

A choking noise, a clatter, and I scrambled for the table. More noise overhead—thank the *gods*, now I was grateful for the entire sorry lot of them dragging my keel— turned into running feet, but the assassin made another soft, helpless noise.

A gleam over the dark shoulder rose, a pale face.

His eyes burning, his hair mussed, my *s'tarei* wrenched my own largest knife free and plunged it into the assassin's other kidney. His hand came up, cupping the chin, and as I blurted "No, for questioning—" he made a convulsive cracking movement, and the body slid through his hands.

That was the moment Janaire reached the top of the stairs and whispered a globe of soft silver glow—*zaradai*, a witchlight— into existence, sending it into the air with a quick, practiced flick of her wrist, effectively destroying my night-vision. I swore foully, my hip bumping the table and sending it along the floor with a screech.

"How many?" D'ri, in clear, harsh G'mai.

"What in the name of—" Redfist's bellow from overhead.

I shook my head, Darik arrived at my side, and I restrained the urge to reach for his knife. "Don't know," I snapped.

Atyarik loomed behind Janaire, his hair a wild mess and a fire in his Tyaanismir gaze promising trouble to any of the assassin's cohorts.

"Kaia?" Redfist. No Gavrin, and no piping of Diyan's voice.

"*Check the boy, Redfist!*" I yelled up the stairs, tradetongue harsh against my tongue, and grabbed the three-legged table. I half-turned, meaning to search the kitchen, but Darik's hand closed over my shoulder.

"Wait."

"If there are more—"

"Then they are long gone. Or just as dead as this one." His chin lifted slightly. "Tyaanismir?"

Atyarik arrived at the stair-foot, tossed something— harness straps, two hilts, D'ri's blades—to my *s'tarei*, and half-turned as Janaire ran, velvet-foot, down in his wake. "With the princess, J'na."

She nodded, sending the witchlight spinning, and I realized I was naked save for baffle and breeches, clutching a table, and could have been killed if not for Darik. I sagged against the wall for a moment, ignoring the cold, and let out a long, comfortingly obscene term I had learned in Hain.

And at that moment, yes, I *definitely* wished for kafi.

WORTH THE COIN

D'RI AND ATYARIK SEARCHED THE house from roof to cellar; Redfist and Ninefinger slipped out to examine the courtyard and the outer wall. Gavrin, of course, we knew was not dead, for he was snoring with abandon, audible even through the door, and barely stirred when Redfist eyed his room. The barbarian caught sight of a flicker of movement and had almost bellowed, but found it was Diyan, one hand out-flung, beside the Pesh lutebanger.

He had found a warm place to sleep after all.

A babe in arms, that one, Redfist had said, with the ghost of a smile, before he had shut the front door, and he could have meant either of them.

I searched the assassin's corpse while Janaire lit candles and kindled a lamp, letting the *zaradai* wink out with a rueful expression, rubbing at her temples as if it pained her.

Two new-moon knives, stilettes and lockpicks as well. Small sealed clay cylinders of differing sizes—poisons, or acids, or navthen-and-ortrox to spark a flame. A dark cloth wound about the head—not black, for that makes one more conspicuous at night, but a well-worn deep blue. When I unwound the *dhabri*, carefully, I found a young Antai woman, her head lolling strangely on its broken stem of a neck, her teeth painted with semtar so no gleam would betray her location. I propped her mouth open with a knifehilt and found the poison tooth—back right molar, still intact—and settled to searching her clothing more thoroughly. A length of flexible wire with handles— garrotte, and a finely made one at that—and various other odds and ends.

No thin inkmarks upon her chest, or on the inside of her thigh. She was Antai, she was not Shainakh.

She was not a Hand.

When I glanced up, Janaire had her fingers pressed to her mouth. In the wavering lamplight, she looked very young. "Is it another?" she whispered, the blur of her lowlander accent softening the words into a child's intonation.

"Not a Shainakh." I tried to sound reassuring. "I was certain nobody in Antai wishes me dead *this* badly."

"And now?"

G'mai threatened to burn my throat, so I forced myself to speak softly and slowly in tradetongue, to give myself time to think. "It is not at all characteristic for the Guild to send a blackback to the wrong house. Bad for business." *What did I do when I was here last? Nothing too drastic. There was that priest, and the tree-gems. Oh, and those two port guards. Neither of them were merchant-noble.*

"There is a guild?"

"Thieves and assassins. The Council wants peace in the streets, purse-cutters and throat-cutters want to make a living. Business works best that way." *Like every other city. Pesh has no Guild, but they have their hungry god.* I felt along the body's calf, found another knifehilt. "Ah, now. This is something."

"What is it?" Janaire shivered, pulling her shawl more tightly. It was silk, of course, and its weave was peculiarly stippled, marking it as G'mai instead of Kshanti or Hain fabric. The fringe was very fine, too, and I wondered once more why she was so determined to stay outside

99

G'maihallan's borders. "Assassins have a guild? It does not seem..."

"Not quite polite. But profitable." *And the infighting is enough to keep them mostly occupied.* I carefully tugged at the hilt with two fingers, and it slid free with distressing ease. Was it oiled, or smeared with poison in some oily base? "Mother's *tits*," I breathed, tipping the short, thin blade this way and that. The hilt was plain and leather-wrapped, but the curve of the guards and the etching along the flat would tell me much. "Bring the lamp closer."

Footsteps, then. I played the light along the blade as D'ri and Atyarik reappeared. My shoulders drew tight with cold, henflesh spreading from my nape down either side of my spine. Three angular glyphs, two of them married at a stem—that would be her use-name, given by her sponsor. The last glyph was three curved lines meaning *smoke* in the Pensar symbol-language, carved deeply into the foundation block of every temple those cruel, pale conquerors laid. It was always seen with another oddly scratched and twisted mark, one no Antai native, from merchant to hinterland peasant, from Port Guard to lowly Guild pickpocket, rouged Featherseller or common street daub, would pronounce, even as a loan-word.

Death. It is a slippery, sinuous word in Pensar, and held to be great unluck to voice. They use instead a term borrowed from the ruins of Corthuar, something like *breath-halt-choke.* Still, the Pensari death-word looms behind that smoke-glyph like thunder behind lightning.

My braids felt lopsided, from sleep and combat. I shook my head as the front door creak-groaned its opening song. Redfist was a shadow, his odiferous friend looming behind him. "Nothing, K'ha." Weariness tinged the shortening of my name, and I suspected he was fighting back a yawn. "What have we here, then?"

"A junior member of *Shandua-hua.* The Smoke Clan." I settled on my haunches, repressing the urge to hunch my shoulders protectively. "Thank the Moon it wasn't a full-grown viper."

"Assassin." Muscle flickered on D'ri's chest and shoulders as he crouched too, examining the body and the assorted implements ranged neatly on the floor. His heat touched my own bare arm, and the blond giant Ninefinger piped up.

"Lass, here." He began plucking at his shirt, and I glanced at him curiously. His name was strange—he had all ten of his digits—but the explanation for it was an ancestor who had wrestled some sort of reeking beast in the far north and lived to tell of it, losing only a finger. "Catch your death, ye will."

A bit late for that. "I am well enough." My torn shirt lay on the floor too, crumpled and bloody. The shallow slice along my forearm was already clotted fast, and G'mai do not worry overmuch on the wound-rot. The antiseptic property in our blood is a gift from the Moon, and I was confident now that the little assassin's blades had not been painted. Besides, the Moon grants our people some various immunities to the venoms of the world. "Simply very, very curious why one of their sprats would be sent after *me*. It is almost insulting."

Atyarik bent, touched the corpse's chin with one long finger, tilted her face into the light. "A waste."

Very young, a scar on her upper lip and her dark hair cropped short as a Pesh bondslave's. I did not like to think upon what might have driven her into the viper-nest—poverty, vengeance, sheer ill-luck. "At least the Shan do not poison their promise-blades," I murmured.

Darik's hand closed on my wrist. I let him examine the slice, and his jaw hardened. "I do not like this."

"No *s'tarei* would." I reclaimed my arm and forced my knees to unbend, combat-weariness settling in my bones. *Now* I wanted to go back to bed. "'Tis a very good thing I could not sleep."

"Kaia?" Janaire's brow was creased. "I have a thought."

"Oh?"

"Are you so certain...forgive me, but are you absolutely certain this blade was meant for you?"

I considered it, and the blond barbarian let out a muffled curse, his head lost in his shirt. He seemed determined to strip. Well, D'ri and I were both simply in trews, perhaps it was a custom of theirs to bare their chests when their hosts were threatened. D'ri rose too, slowly, and the scar at his throat was glaringly visible even in this dim light. An assassin had reached the heart of the Dragaemir palace and attempted to remove his head with a garrotte, he said, and that was a troubling table indeed. It would have to be a long arm to stretch this far, but with enough coin, many things are possible.

Yet a scar-lipped snakelet not even old enough to lay eggs...now that I had my wits working, I had a dismal feeling I knew who had sent her.

"We shall see." I realized I had spoken in G'mai, repeated it in tradetongue.

"Here." Ninefinger offered me his shirt. It was big enough to reach my knees, and perhaps he wished to be kind, or generous, but the cloth was rough and I had no desire to smell like him.

I shook my head. "No need. We must set the body outside the gate before dawn."

"Outside? But—" Janaire protested, and Atyarik said, "We shall not bury or—" at the same moment.

I silenced them both with a look. "Tis the custom, in this place. And," I added thoughtfully, "it will signal that if they wish to come for me, or anyone else in this house, they had best send someone worth the coin."

AS A REED

PEARL-CLOUD MORNGLOW FELL THROUGH small, thick glass panes; the window was probably older than Atyarik. D'ri, the glow picking out blue-black highlights in his hair and touching his tight-knotted shoulders under silk and leather, polished the hilts of his *dotanii* and showed a small portion of his cheek. I yawned, blinking, and calculated the angle of the light. "Tis past dawn."

"You needed rest." He did not turn. Arms folded across his chest, his back very straight, his boots resting precisely as if he expected an attack at any moment.

Perhaps he did. His inflection was still intimate, but his tone was only slightly less than forbidding. It was a strange and uneasy pairing.

I asked you to wake me, if I did not wake myself. Irritation served no purpose, so I aimed for diplomacy. For once. "As did you."

"Mh." A light noise, neither affirmation nor denial. "The body vanished."

"Ah." I stretched, luxuriously. The bedstead was old, but a fresh mattress and clean linen will make any pile of ancient timber a comfortable nest. "Now *that* is interesting."

"How so?"

"If she had failed on proper business, they would leave it at the gate as a warning to expect more." I rolled up to sitting, tested my arm. Only the usual aches in my joints and muscles, and the scratch looked a few days instead of hours old. Janaire's healing was a wonder. "As it is, perhaps she thought to take matters into her own hands, or made a mistake. We should see no more of the Shan. Especially after today."

"Ah, yes. Your errand." He still did not turn. "Tell me again why it is so necessary."

"I would prefer to know, instead of guess." I drew my knees up, clasped my arms about them. Both legs and arms were livid-bruised from stone. "D'ri?"

"Hm?" Another short sound.

"Do you think it likely tis related to your scar?"

He did not stiffen, but I felt the shortness of his breath in my own chest. "We are at some distance from G'maihallan."

"That is no answer, *s'tarei'mi*." I rubbed gently at the slice on my forearm with my fingertips. "Serves me right, afoot without a weapon."

"I wondered at that."

"I could not sleep. I thought perhaps to brew some *kafi* and think."

He nodded. "I...am sorry I did not wake as well."

"You were exhausted, D'ri." I used the gentlest inflection possible. "And you were quick enough when the battle began."

"It troubles me."

"Do not." I hesitated, slid my bare legs off the bed, and winced slightly at the cool wooden floor. Perhaps a cartload of sweetrush would help downstairs, and buskins. I found my second-best shirt, pulled it over my head to at least keep some warmth in, and padded to the window.

He stared down at the side-garden and the wall beyond, jaw set and eyes half-lidded. A fine profile, the

Dragaemir harshness with enough youth to soften the cheekbones—but not *too* much. I closed my hand about his shoulder, tentatively. "D'ri." As softly as possible. "Do not trouble yourself. You dispatched the threat handily enough." I was about to add I had been too mazed with lack of sleep to take proper precautions, but he glanced at me, and a scalding flush ran from my cold feet to the top of my half-undone braids.

"Perhaps I am not quite a failure as a *s'tarei*, then."

"Ah." It was, I decided, faintly amusing we both thought in the same channels. "What a pair we make, each feeling unworthy of the other. Do you suppose others feel thus?"

His chin settled, somewhat stubbornly. "I would not know."

"I think it likely." I held his gaze. "I should have stayed in Anjalismir, perhaps. Waited. For you." My throat was very dry, and morning in my mouth was not as foul as leftover hanta, but foul enough.

"I should have disobeyed the Queen and left." He shook his head slightly. "I am of a mind to no longer be dutiful."

Did he truly think one of the People would set assassins on him? To kill a *s'tarei* is to kill an *adai*, and to kill an *adai* is the only crime there is no forgiveness for within G'maihallan's borders. And yet, the scar glared at his throat. "Of all the terms I could use to describe you, *dutiful* is...well, perhaps it does suit." I used the term for a slightly balky animal that had good reason to protest, with the slight lift at the end that made it affectionate.

His lips curved slightly. I watched them, and the certainty that I could rise on my toes, lean forward, and he would more than meet me halfway froze me in place.

I am accustomed to tolerating such attentions, and nothing more. To feel the other side of that coin was...disturbing. There was none of the softness of

Kesamine's bed, or the moonturn or so I had accompanied a male Rjiin courtesan on a caravan to Shaitush. He had been slim-muscled, flexible, and of a pliant nature, that one, but possessed of good business sense and a wry wit. I had gone through the motions of physical joining out of curiosity. Nothing in me stirred even to such an artist's attentions, and he ruefully admitted he had tried his best. *Perhaps elvish women are different,* he had said, and even though I hated that word, I had laughed. I had not told him of the twinning—why bother? And a lack of the bodily urges that seemed to make such a fine mess of the people in every city was welcome, for it meant I was thinking with a clarity they did not possess.

Now, being subject to the yearning and the heat was uncomfortable, distracting, and downright *dangerous*. It could so easily be used against me.

The moment passed, I leaned away ever so slightly from Darik's equally small shifting of his weight. Strangely, his smile widened. "Shall I become as a reed, for thee?"

It had been a long, long time since I had heard any of the courtship songs, and I found myself smiling as well. "And bend in the wind as the mountains cry." An open, unguarded moment, and for that small space, I saw him as he could have been, a young *s'tarei* in the first honey-flush of bonding. Hawk-proud, kitten-playful, and hopeful as the flowers that break through snow at the end of winter's long grasp on the slopes of stone-teeth rising above Anjalismir's main Keep.

The moment passed, and I squeezed his shoulder, gently. "Breakfast. And we should be gone before too long, morning is the best time."

He nodded. His breath, his shoulders, and his expression had all eased. He caught my wrist as I turned away, his thumb feathering over the sensitive underside, where even muscle from daily drill could not hide a softness. I halted, and he lifted my hand. Pressed a kiss into my callused palm, seeming not to care about the roughness. "Thank you, *adai'mi*."

"I did nothing." But I did not tug to free myself. "I will need you today, D'ri. Bring breakfast, I do not care to visit the thieves with an empty belly."

"I thought you fought better a little hungry."

"This is no duel, *s'tarei'mi*." I closed my fingers, still feeling the print of his lips inside the hollow of my hand.

"And thank the Moon for that," was his parting shot. "I could not survive another."

I waved him away, and set myself to dress and untangle my recalcitrant braids.

All the time, my hand burned, and when he had left to go downstairs I pressed my own mouth against my palm, closing my eyes and pretending, for just a moment, that I could be what he needed.

HEAD OF
MANY BODIES

THE CUSTOMS HOUSE IS A Pensari palace, shouldering the wharfside warehouses aside and gleaming dully. It lays claim to being the Khan Altai's last home, but that dubious honor is more likely given to the pile of slowly-rotting Pensari spongestone set on the crown of Low Hatha'huan'ara Hill. They called that malevolent stone nest "the Diadem" when they spoke of it at all, and it is said to be cursed; even though the space around it was valuable enough, it was not crowded with shanties or villas. It lays bare and weed-blown; pale vaporous lights can occasionally be seen in the arrowslits after dark. None admit to knowing who kindle any sort of flame in that spine-broken heap. Some whisper that the Pensar gods of night and ice were still worshipped there secret, by those who wished for vengeance or gain.

Between the Customs House and the Diadem, nestled in the Chuabrhua'lath, there is a large counting-house with red-painted walls and a throbbing tavern in one corner, and that is where one goes if one has business with the Guild. The Chua teems with stink, filth, and scrabble. Its full name means, as far as is translatable, the Naked Anus.

The smell alone will tell you why.

The street-crowds around the Naharl'lath—the Crimson Hole, as the Guild's home is called—are as orderly as a mass of perpetually tired, dusty, profit-seeking people can be. The streetstalls and shops pay handsomely for the privilege of operating around the Naharl, but profit as well. The reward has to be substantial, because proof of trafficking in stolen property was worth a spell in the gaols. Should a streetstall or shop owner be unlucky enough to be dragged gaol-ward, they would find protection from the other prisoners supplied by the Guild, and their businesses taken in hand until their release. The Guard did not like to draw too close to the Hole, and who could blame them?

I pierced the crowds, Darik in my wake, my left hand almost cramping from the strain of holding my fingers in the accepted manner. An outsider found copying the Guild signs is usually stripped and dangled from a roof on the first offense, and that is enough to dissuade most, even rich or noble brats who wish to appear dangerous to their fellows.

The second offense is not forgiven.

Steps worn into a curve by the passage of generations of feet led to the Smalldoor, a high-arched aperture lined with sun-yellow tiles. I closed my eyes, followed the steps by memory, so I was not blinded by the sudden dimness inside. There was a soft whisper of blade leaving sheath; my hand blurred out and locked the child's wrist, stripping the knife from him as an afterthought. "Not today, little one." The ceremonial greetings of Antai's Guild are full of Pensar loan-words, a curious mumbling dialect I had not mastered much beyond the basics of.

I took the rest of the small cave, nominally a tavern, in one glance. The Keeper was a new face; perhaps old, fat Curajoh had retired to a villa. In different corners, eyes gleamed, and blades as well. The fire was low; the heat is the first test. In summer there is a blaze, in winter there is not, to teach the young thieves discomfort is inevitable. I stamped twice upon the threshold, warning them I had a companion who was not of the Guild and that I vouched for him, and pushed the tiny door-guard—a thin, obviously part-Kmeri scrap of a boy too small for the down sprouting on his upper lip—away, but not overly harshly. He moved backward without looking, his feet in soft buskins, his head wrapped with a black cloth as well. If he did well at the door, he would likely graduate to the daily harvest, picking pockets in the great markets or wharfside.

"Who's that a-knocking?" A deep rumble from the bar at the left back corner, a massive curlicued piece of driftwood rumored to have washed onshore during the Storm Years.

"A traveler on a moonlit road," I replied. D'ri pressed behind me, but I did not move, letting them take a good eyeful of me.

"And where are you bound, traveler?"

There was no mead or ale at that bar. Here past the Smalldoor, there is only a massive cabinet behind the Keeper, its many drawers holding herb, tincture, paste, and other things. Some drawer-fronts are marked, others are not, and it takes many years before a young Keeper is allowed to mix or mingle, decant or stopper.

Given the nature of the substances, that is for the best.

"For the dells or the eyrie, Keeper of the Many Deaths. I am Kaia Steelflower, and I have business here." In short, I would go to whatever part of the House I needed in order to find an answer.

A short silence, gratifying enough, before the Keeper breathed a term of passing obscenity and his large white hands—delicate and pampered, for they are the most valuable part of his brethren—flickered in the gloom. "Ah. Come in, come in. You and your friend are welcome here. Hospitality is offered."

Well, at least we won't be knifed in the House. "Many thanks." I pressed my palms together, bowed slightly, and set off down the internal steps, avoiding the third out of habit. D'ri followed, stepping only where I did as if he was an apprentice, and a murmur ran below the surface of the silence.

There was a patter of running feet. Someone was being alerted to my presence. I halted in the middle of a bare expanse of floor, feeling an unfriendly gaze, and turned my head slightly.

"*Sorche!*" the Keeper hissed. Now I could see he was bald, and his pate gleamed with oil, stippled with inkneedle marks in whorls meant to catch and hold both knowledge and luck.

Now that was a familiar name.

"Ahi-a," I said, very softly. "Out of the egg now, smoke-bitch?"

She wore a dark *dhabri*, wrapped and knotted in some barbaric fashion, almost like the Banath of the Far East, those figments of G'mai children's night terrors. Perhaps she had adopted the style to cover the pale streak in her curly hair, or simply affected it to set herself apart. Her knuckles were white, and if she kept moving that steadily toward me, I would have to draw a knife.

"Business." A slight lisp colored the word. There was a hard dart of light—perhaps she had acquired a false tooth, to replace the one knocked free years ago. "Returned to finish our duel, foreigner?"

"We have no duel, Smahua Sorche-*va*." What were the odds of me seeing the one Shanhua I had a tale or two of history with, here? Had she had heard of my arrival and dropped an indiscreet word, perhaps thinking a student could succeed where Sorche's own sponsor and thiefmother had failed, then come to wait for me? It was just the sort of ill-considered action I would expect from

111

the journeyman she had been, not from a full assassin in her own right.

Another shadow detached itself from the gloom, and there was a quick movement. My hand twitched, I felt D'ri tense, but it was another thief, this one far too small to be anything but an apprentice. "No," said a small, piping little boy's voice, and I thought of Diyan. "Hospitality, *maneft' lua.*"

Thiefmother. So she was training little poisoners, now. A position of high prestige, but it also kept her squarely in the Guild's sight. It was not at all usual for the Smoke Clan to let one of their own serve in the Red House. The Many-fingered and the Fish-eye clans were those who traditionally trained any who wished to take the thief's way in Antai, and they are jealous of the prerogative. Thievery training is the accepted first school for those who wish to join the assassins, and freelancers are requested to earn membership by passing the basic thief-tests and bringing a greater dowry-gift to the Guild.

The Twins, the Guild are sometimes called, or the Twin Excrescences. The assassin clans claim to be the elder sibling, but the thieving clans laugh and say *what is an assassin but a thief of breathing life?*

Uniting such a collection of light-fingered, murderous groups called for a special touch. The Clanmothers, however—some are male, but even they are named *Matrihua*, Mother, by their clan-children—understand that peace is more profitable, even if less immediately satisfying. Decisions which cannot be collectively reached, or negotiations requiring a titular ruler, are left with the Head.

I waited. The Keeper hissed something else in their argot, and I caught a word or two. Yes, I was expected.

How very interesting.

"You killed my mother, *Steelflower.*" She dragged the third syllable, turning it into a relative of the word for a blacksmith's slagpile. I had not suspected such poetry in her. "And I swear, by—"

"Cease." A new voice, this one quiet but with an undertone of authority that halted Sorche maddeningly just out of range. "You do not hold the iron to back such a threat, Smahua's get." A thock of a staff on uneven wooden flooring, and I knew who it had to be.

I did not take my gaze from Sorche, but I placed my palms together again. "A great honor to hear the words of *Ban-juae*," I said, respectfully enough, even though the term could be taken as an insult.

On some days, the one titled the Head of Many Bodies might take offense at the name. On most, however, he would take it as the honor due his achievements, and it would even amuse him.

A gamble, to address him thus, and one I often took.

A wheezing laugh, another staff-strike. A faint jingling that would be the bell-bracelets he wore on either wrist. "Kaahua-kaahaiua." Two words, one the spreading of a courtesan's legs, the other a plaintive cry of seabirds. So he remembered the poetry contests. I had not done too badly, though Antai's dialect is slippery indeed. "It is we who are honored. Come, the chai will grow cold."

I measured Sorche—a long, slow, insolent look—then deliberately stepped forward. For a few fractions of a moment I was within her reach, and had she moved...

She did not, and D'ri followed me, his tension intensifying. If she thought to strike at my back, a fully trained *s'tarei* would prove an impediment indeed.

Sorche made a soft inarticulate noise, but she did not move. Now that she knew I was in Antai, I would have to be careful. Not too much for my own sake, since she ached to defeat me before she killed, but for those I...cared for.

A snake will bite when threatened, but human vipers are not nearly so charitable.

I drew even with the bar, nodded to the Keeper. "If any of my companions suffer sudden ill-health, Sorche of the Smoke, I shall look for you."

She said nothing. The bright beam of her hate burrowed into my back and found no purchase.

The Head's gray robes—of fine quality, despite their artful tattering—fluttered slightly. He tipped his head, turning for the stairs almost hidden behind the Keeper's twisted, polished wharf, and the bandage over his eyes was more than customary or training, or affectation.

He was one of the greatest thief-assassins in Antai's history, the only male Head in a hundred summers or so, and had been born blind.

HOSPITALITY

THE ROOM HAD NOT CHANGED. Wide and full of sunlight from the square crystalline blocks set in the roof, its wooden floor polished to a soft beautiful glow. At the far wall was a tiny lacquered Clau cabinet, its lines verging on the edge of florid, nicely balanced against a curve of wet-black Hain pottery holding the wild arc of a *tamil* branch. The leaves were deeply serrated, flame-colored, and worked against the pottery's simplicity and the cabinet's almost-tastelessness. The pottery was probably worth two or three of the cabinet, and that could have been one of his tests.

It is not enough to steal, he was fond of saying. *You must know* what *you are stealing.*

A lean brown man in rag-serrated gray robes, his slim staff not bothering to sweep the floor before him now that he was on familiar ground, Hoeri-kin Hansate motioned us into his sanctum. "I admit," he said, in heavily accented tradetongue, "I am surprised." He lifted one hand to touch the band over his eye sockets. I knew what lay underneath—filmed, webbed, gray orbs, withering from some disease or blight. The rest of him was hale enough; very few survived underestimating him. He freed his ungaze, letting desiccated sclera, iris, and pupil breathe, and tucked the covering band into a pocket with a quick flick of long, graceful fingers.

I moved a single step to the side, glanced at D'ri. "I doubt that, *han-fua*." The highest title an outsider could give a male Antai rolled off my tongue, as if I had practised it since our last meeting. I was briefly pleased by that. He often shrugged at bloodshed, but did not abide impoliteness of any stripe. *Manners, manners*, he had used to say, tapping one finger on a *benjua* board before he decided he liked poetry contests with a G'mai even better.

So did I. *Benjua* is arcane, boring, and tilted in favor of whoever moves first. It was no wonder the Head played it so often.

A twitch at one corner of his thin, dry-lipped mouth turned his face into a Clau imp-carving for a brief moment. "Your accent has improved. Please, bring your friend to our table. Does he drink chai?"

"He would be honored." I could even be relatively certain the chai was not poisoned.

"And you speak for him?" The question, with its intonation dipping in the middle, asked a subtle question— *as mother, as lover, as thief?*

"My *adai* is familiar with your ways." Darik, low and pleasant, in passable tradetongue. The cadence of G'mai wore through it, a familiar face under a mask. "I am a poor barbarian, and afraid of making some misstep."

"Ah, a man unafraid to admit as much." The Head laughed, a merry dry insect-whisper cackle. "You bring me such interesting things, K'ahnua." It was the word for an eldest daughter, one a merchant does not wish to marry off because she has a good head for counting. Which meant he was extremely pleased—or being sarcastic.

Either was likely. Or both. And now I did not have to answer what precisely D'ri was to me, but the old man perhaps would think in such terms as marriage. *You should marry into a clan, K'aiaha*, he had said once, after a long night of playing *benjua*. I had almost snorted an inelegant laugh before I realized he had meant it kindly, in the manner of a merchant showing great favor to a most promising, albeit foreign, employee.

"Your time is precious. I would not waste it, unless you will it so." I motioned D'ri along, telling him with a glance that he need not step precisely where I did now.

"I have never found fault with your manners." He indicated a low chai-table made of a single block of spongestone, its porous surface decorated with spreading patterns of tea-rings and other splashes. Much business was conducted at this table. "Please, sit. Your house was troubled last night." He folded down, slowly, perhaps playing at age-creaking bones.

Or perhaps not.

"It was," I agreed. "Though that is not the only reason for my visit."

"Hm." An iron kettle hung over a faint depression in the stone, steaming gently—the water was freshly boiled. The familiar ritual of making chai absorbed him for a few moments, enough time for me to settle on the other side of the table. "You are not behind in your tithes."

"No." I restrained myself from adding *of course not*.

He stirred, sniffing carefully. Some said he could smell fear or untruth. Or sarcasm. "Our family grows restive."

In that case, what is a Shan-hua doing downstairs with the little ones? "Such is their nature."

A series of small nods, a doddering old man's movement, but far too fluid. "You remember my words well. Tell me, K'ahnua, why you did not take Sorche's life?"

It was an unexpected question, so I paused before answering. "Before, or now?"

"Either."

"I do not murder children." *Not if I can help it.* And, thank the Moon, I had not ever been forced to such an expedient.

"Is she still a child?" Bright interest, his mouth opening slightly, filmed gaze moving as if it followed an invisible thing through the room. He took his time selecting the bowl from the rack cut on the host's side of the table; his fingers lingered over glazed or unglazed porcelain, searching for the perfect pairing. He finally selected a shallow *bu-yan* of very fine Clau whitestone, the precious almost-translucent material they do not sell anymore. They have not mined it for many a year indeed, so any instance of *kalallallillanuharala*—such is their name for it, the Shainakh call it *albestrkha*—is precious. Kesamine has a teardrop of it, hung at her throat with black silk on feast and Festival days, worth almost as much as her inn.

"Some are such their entire lives." Unease touched my nape. My braids were very heavy, because my neck was taut as towship-cable, hauling a weight behind it on the water's resisting back.

He whisked the chai in a rustic wooden mixbowl, its spice rising with steam in perfect curls. "The world has changed, Flower-of-Metal. The Clans grow jealous. Many outsiders have come."

Well, Antai has a port. "The ships keep bringing them."

A faint hint of sour amusement touched his lips, an expression he wore often during poetry contests. "And many come from the North, bearing strange tidings."

"I have never traveled very far north from Antai." *Redfist's friend? Why send a half-trained snakelet, then?*

"Are you about to?" He set the whisk aside, poured with a steady hand into the glowing, innocent *bu-yan*.

"I leased a villa." Meaning, *I intend to winter here.* To add that it was halfway up a Hill could have been mistaken for boasting, so I did not.

"With good red Shainakh gold. Luck favors you lately."

Well, the news would travel quickly. "Perhaps."

"You have become wiser. When last we quoted Simyaua together, your answer would have been *for now*."

Simyaua was fond of adages that showed just how quickly luck could turn rank, and how the only truly happy man was one who had died without misfortune. I did not answer. The message was clear enough.

The Head lifted the bowl, savored a mouthful, and passed it to me with the slight bow tradition demanded from a host. I took it, scorch-warm against my palms, and his index finger tapped mine twice.

Tiny, leathery touches, and they echoed hollowly in the well of my belly.

One, two. *Dear gods.*

The chai was sweet, strong as they took it in Antai with no milkfat. Sometimes they add a dollop of boiled and whipped *cras* oil, especially for the harbor lifters. It keeps those rope-muscled bravos warm even on sleet-lashed stormdays, hauling cargo in and out of deep, malodorous holds. I took a goodly mouthful, passed it to D'ri, and sweat began along the curve of my lower spine. I studied the Head's racked, copper-skinned features.

"Smahua's thiefchild will be chastised for her inhospitable behavior." A glint of steel in his tone, soft and subtle, the hidden blade.

Ah. So it was Sorche. Why would she send a...oh. "Perhaps Sorche's apprentice was simply impatient."

"The young often are." He accepted my graciousness with a small nod, but his mouth had turned down at the corners. "The Keeper has your chits, so the merchants do not cheat you overmuch. Do you wish what you left in my care?"

Why else would I come? "Yes. I thank you, *han-fua*."

"Ah, she *thanks* me. Tell me, friend-of-the-Flower, do you enjoy the chai?"

D'ri glanced at me. He looked interested, a bland expression he probably wore during interminable protocol-laced events in the Dragon Palace's great bulk. I have only seen paintings of the great city of the People and the house of royalty at its center, with the holy mountain containing Beleriaa's tomb rising above.

"It is very sweet, and very good," he said finally, soft careful tradetongue struggling to match the rise and fall of a tongue trained to subtle inflections and cadences.

"You have an accent." The Head nodded, that same doddering movement, a wicked cast to his mouth now. "Where is your homeland?"

"Far across the sea." Darik glanced at me, and the Head made a soft *tch*ing sound.

"That is all she would ever say, either. Now, leave me. There is much business today, I have had all the leisure I am allowed."

"Winds grant you luck," I murmured, and sitting still for long enough to be polite was a torment, my knees pressing into wood and the consciousness of something very, very wrong indeed looming above me. I *had* to act reluctant to quit his company, especially since he honored me so singularly.

Downstairs, the Keeper did not even glance at me, but one of his silent assistants slid a thin trashmetal chain holding several jingling brass tabs across the counter—marks that I was a member of the Guild in good standing, and could be overcharged only at some peril. I thanked him with a nod—the chest-cache I'd left with the Head was probably already at the villa.

I would have to be very careful, opening it.

Kaia? Darik, the *taran-adai* very faint and faraway inside the bonecase of my skull, struggling against the current of my thoughts.

I motioned him along, and he obeyed. We did not speak for a long while.

I was not quite sure it was safe.

DISTRUSTFUL OF AIR

A SMALL, FILTHY ALLEY IN the middle of the heaving press of the docks swallowed us without a sound. I was fairly sure we were not followed by now, and pulled D'ri aside, against the wall. "Listen." The word carried a great deal of urgency in G'mai, my tongue dry and my palms a little damper than I liked. "Can you sense any pursuit?"

He shook his head. "They watched us as we left. Now..." He tilted his head, the fierce killing quiet of a *s'tarei* closing around him. "No, I do not think so. What is it, Kaialitaa?"

The name—*little brave one*, with the added accent that made it a tiny jeweled sharpness, like a decorative needle or stilette—should have pained me. I was too worried to feel the cut. "The little viper last night was Sorche's apprentice. It is very likely she heard Sorche curse my name and set out to avenge her. And yet."

"And yet?"

I took a deep breath, ignoring the stench and leaning against the filthy, crumbling wall of a fish-crammed warehouse. "There are two of us in danger."

He did not argue, simply leaned close, examining my face. A frown was probably cutting deep furrows across my forehead, down my chin, casting nets from the corners of my eyes.

Janaire frowned very prettily. I shook the thought away, a quick motion I used to check over his shoulder. Still clear enough. No rasping along my nerves, but I was shaken enough to see pursuers where none existed.

"The old man?" What light managed to pierce the alley's depth showed his dawning comprehension. "Of course."

I could still feel the two dry, light taps on my finger. "Not the little one, and not Gavrin. Janaire and Atyarik, is there any...?"

"They were simply searching for me. Perhaps news of my good fortune has reached the Queen." The traditional term to state a young *s'tarei* had found his *adai* carried no bitter tinge; his tone was merely thoughtful. Blue-black hair fell across his forehead, and I longed to brush it away.

I denied that longing. "But to kill an *adai*..." I exhaled sharply. Even if we were overheard in some fashion, I could be certain there were only four people in Antai who understood my native tongue. And half of them were in this alley.

"I had reached an age past expecting an *adai*." He glanced up, checking the crooked slice of sky the alley permitted. I waited, but he simply stared, unseeing. "Perhaps my royal aunt thought so too, and thought to cut a tapestry string before it snarled."

"The G'mai we met in Vulfentown cannot have carried word beyond the Seven Reaches yet," I pointed out. "'Tis Redfist's new friend who has the key to this riddle." I used the word for a murderous misstep on a mountain pass, and his slight, pleased smile was a reward I did not deserve. Puns, riddles, a turn of phrase, a well-chosen utterance—our bards and tale-spinners are held in high honor, and the speed with which they can flay pride and lay open the heart of a matter is legendary.

His expression changed. For a moment I thought he would lean closer...but instead, his gaze focused on my forehead. "Why the large red one as well, then?"

The same thing had occurred to me; I told the tiny cheated feeling at the very back of my throat to go away. "There was some trouble in his homeland. He says he came through Antai before." It was a thin explanation at best. "Redfist would have warned us if there was a commission on him in Antai. If he knew."

Then again, I had thought Ammerdahl Rikyat would never have sought to mislead me, too. It was enough to make a sellsword suspicious. Of course, we are even distrustful of the air we breathe, or so the proverb goes. I found myself studying the band of scarring at D'ri's throat. At least I could be certain of a *s'tarei*.

No. At least, I could be certain of *him*.

He shook his head slightly, his throat moving as he spoke. "I do not like this."

"Nor do I. Come, we should—" I moved as if to urge him along; I disliked the thought of tarrying now we knew we were clear of pursuit and in agreement.

His hands clasped my shoulders, and he kissed me. A pleasant pressure of lips, the dance of tongues, and again the dangerous softness rose to swamp me. Was this what the courtship songs were about? It was too intense to be *safe*. Yet there was a curious comfort in the blindness of trust.

A whip cracked, horses heaving as a cart rumbled past the mouth of the alley, and I jolted back into my own skin. His forehead rested against mine, our breathing following the same high, fast rhythm.

It is the blood-heat, only that. Was it normal to shake? Was this what Janaire felt, when Atyarik touched her? What my mother had felt, when my father drew near? I had a vague memory of being carried on his chest as he followed my mother during her duties as the Heir of Anjalismir. I

123

remembered resting my cheek against his *dotanii* straps, all well with the world and my mother's light lilting laughter soothing us both.

"Kaia," Darik breathed. I shut my eyes, just for a moment, and leaned against him.

Then I stepped away, wishing I did not feel so bereft once his heat no longer reached me. Still, he followed, and that was enough.

Reckoned for It

"KAIA!" REDFIST CALLED IN GREETING, I did not halt. Ninefinger glanced up, his ill-luck eyes widening, but by then I was moving quickly, my boots slapping flagstone floor, and I kicked the chair from beneath him. Wood groan-creaked, and D'ri was suddenly *there*, catching Redfist's shoulder and pushing him back into his chair's embrace, whispering fiercely in the red barbarian's ear.

Ninefinger's face slammed into the tabletop, knocking over two drinking-horns and a chai pot. Mead splashed, a sharp sticky alcoholic fume rising. The table, a long chunk of heavy hinterland oak too bulky to be carried from the villa, seated perhaps fifteen, and quivered all along its length. I grabbed his wrist, twisting, had his meaty arm locked and my palm at his nape, my fingers digging under his filthy, gold-gleaming hair.

I am smaller and much lighter, yes, but there is something to be said for resting a boot on the back of a man's bent knee, and grinding said knee into the flagstones while your arm snake-wriggles under, locks *his* arm uselessly away, and your palm presses upon the nape. There are ways to keep even the heaviest of giants from struggling free, especially when you slide your slimmest, sharpest blade parallel to his throat and use it to point his gaze at the ceiling. Like a young sheep, neck stretched before mutton is served.

Leverage is a concept any thief learns early, and a female sellsword alone in the world even earlier.

"*Kaia!*" Redfist surged up, but D'ri made another quick movement and the red-and-white Skaialan settled just as quickly.

"Barbarian dog." My lips skinned back from my teeth, my tradetongue clearly enunciated in Corran Ninefinger's dirt-ringed ear. I glanced at D'ri, only long enough to see he had Redfist well in hand. "What have you done?"

Darik said something else too low for me to hear, and Redfist let out a grunt, as if he'd been struck. Perhaps he had, I had more than enough work in keeping Ninefinger subdued, and he only quieted when my stilette's edge kissed his throat afresh. The blade was sharp as a whisper, and I could slash one side of his throat neatly enough. The blood would be some trouble to mop up, but that would not be *his* problem. "Come now," I said, softly. "What have you done, and what were you planning to drag my friend Redfist into?"

He said something in Skaialan, harsh consonants and equally harsh vowels, a burr in the back of the throat. The stilette scraped skin, and a line of bright blood formed between wiry golden beard hairs.

I hissed, much like a Smoke clan adder myself. "In tradetongue, dog."

"He says he doesnae know what ye're about, lass." Redfist gave up, settled fully in his chair with a creak. "What is this?"

"Our visitor last night was the first of many." I tightened my hold on the blond giant's greasiness, and he was very still with the blade knocking at his pulse. "What are you wanted for? Tell me now, and I might let you live."

"Lass, let him go." Redfist, it seemed, wished to be a diplomat. "Corran is a *friend*."

Ninefinger babbled more in Skaialan. Perhaps I had knocked the ability to speak tradetongue out of his very large skull. His stink was more heated now, fear-struggle turning him damp and slippery.

"A friend warns when he may bring death to his hosts," I snarled. "Shall I slit his throat, Redfist, or does he explain?"

"He can barely jabber with you holding him li' that." Redfist leaned forward slightly, but Darik tensed. The barbarian subsided, and Corran Ninefinger's babble took on a tone I knew—frantic, seeking to please, to take the whetted blade from the blood trapped under his skin. "Easy, Kaia. He's my friend."

"That does not make him mine. Everyone in this house is in danger, because of *this* lout." I tightened my grasp. It would take some doing and a shifting of my position to snap his neck, he had so much sheer bulk. But I could open the jugular with a single motion from here, should it become necessary.

Redfist folded his hands, staring at Ninefinger. Who had regained his tradetongue, it seemed, for he began to spit disjointed sentences laced with what sounded like nonsense. "Nae, *crannok finnair*...Rainak, *curaigh le shennong—*"

"Nae, Corran." Redfist shook his head, beads braided into his clean, oiled beard clicking. "'Tis past time. Let him go, Kaia. He's nae the one the barstids are after."

"Well, it's not *me*, for once, and Janaire and Atyarik...Gavrin..." My grasp loosened slightly. Perhaps it was a measure of the stinking man-mountain's intelligence that he did not try my grasp.

Patiently, our ruddy Skaialan spread his hands. "'Tis me. I can understand yer anger, lass, but spare him. It's for love of Highlands and clan he's here far from home, and offering me his service. Be angry at *me*, Kaia."

127

"Oh." My grip loosened further, and I hopped aside with a final yank at the man's hair, to remind him I was not to be trifled with. "Well. When were you going to share this information with me, then?"

"I didnae know for sure." His face crumpled slightly, straightened with an effort. His cheeks had turned to blushing apples. "Nor did he."

And if not for Sorche deciding she hated me enough to risk her standing in the Guild, I might not either, until too late. "Well, then." The resultant pause was full of the low crackle of the fire, the villa breathing as afternoon sun-warmth caressed its walls. "I may have been mistaken, Ninefinger." The stiffness of the phrase was intentional; I *did not like* the man, and was happy to have any hook to hang said dislike upon.

"Tis only a broken nose," the blond giant moaned, shaking free a square of rancid cloth from his pocket as he rose, gingerly. Dripping with mead and blood, he wiped at his Festival mask of leering gore. "Were you a man, I would call you to answer for that."

"I shall gladly meet you in the dueling ring, barbarian." I kept the stilette handy, easing away from him. "Issue a challenge, and we shall dance."

"Cafran's *cock*, there will be nae such thing." Redfist heaved himself up, too, and Darik let him. Our barbarian reached for the spilled drinking-horns, broad capable red-furred hands with strangely delicate fingertips. "I had thought I went far enough to escape Black Dunkast." He blinked, heavily, and his upper lip lifted slightly, a gleam of teeth giving the snarl weight.

Darik skirted him and arrived on my side of the table, resting a hand on my shoulder, and the warmth of that contact eased something in me.

"Doon-kiest." I tried the name. "You mentioned him once before, I think."

"Oh, aye. He rules the clans now, with his bastard lot and his treachery." Redfist set the horns aright, carefully, and a shiver of barely repressed fury went through his large frame. His jerkin, large enough to be a whole cow's hide, was only slightly splattered.

The small betraying movement, so uncharacteristic of his usual bluff good temper, was disconcerting. Hinges squeaked at the front of the villa, and if not for a light pleasant tenor working its way through a common Antai drinking-song, I might have drawn my *dotani* to greet the new arrival. It was Gavrin returning from wherever he had roamed, and his tread was merry and light to match the tune. Perhaps Diyan was with him.

Ninefinger pressed the cloth to his abused nose and glared at me.

I well know that look in a man's eye. Sooner or later, the blond giant would try my steel. A good sellsword does not go seeking duels—it wastes time better spent drinking or sleeping—but there are times it is the only possible end to a mutual dislike.

"But more than that," Redfist continued, "he killed my father and destroyed my clan, and one day he will be reckoned for it."

AND HIM THEY
MAY NOT HAVE

THE MINSTREL HELD UP A small jingling bag. "A tavern or two, more will come later when they know me. Fair work, and easy enough, especially with the little one passing a dish to catch raining copper in." He grinned, and Diyan gave a little hop of joy, rattling the wooden bowls he carried. Janaire avoided the boy gracefully, carrying a cauldron with a rag wrapped about its handle. It smelled almost like *qu'anart*, a specialization of lowlander cooks during chill winters, and Atyarik had bread, bought fresh that afternoon. It was as merry a gathering as it could be with Redfist's quiet and his guest's puff-discolored face.

At least the mess had convinced Ninefinger to bathe. He no longer smelled like the bottom of a sweating manure heap.

"So." Janaire set the cauldron down, her fingers flicking. Power rippled, a simple trick to keep the food warm. "I have been a-marketing, and I do not think we have done too badly. Hist, little one, your eating-picks, and some for our guest."

Diyan bolted for the hall to the kitchen, nipping through the door before it could close. A faraway thread of city-noise quieted, the great tide-change between afternoon and dusk spreading through the sky.

D'ri's knee bumped mine under the table. I took a heavy gulp of chai, almost burning my throat. No wine tonight.

I needed a clear head.

"It smells wonderful." Gavrin reached for the ladle, but Janaire slapped lightly at his hand. The Pesh turned crimson, his throat suffusing with bright fire. Atyarik glanced at the minstrel, a faint smile playing about his thin lips. Harsh as the crags of his province, he looked every bit the warmaster to Darik's princeling.

"Kaia." She ladled my bowl first, then D'ri's—a habit I could not break her of. The highest-ranking *adai* is served first, and she persisted in treating me as if I were an elder agemate of hers, due such respect. "*Insh'tai.*"

"*Insh'tai,*" I murmured in return. "There is news."

"Ah." Atyarik set the bread-platter down. "I sensed as much." His gaze flicked to Ninefinger, who glowered at me. It was too much ill-feeling for a simple misunderstanding, but then, his nose *had* been broken, and I had not asked Janaire to gift him with a healing. Nor had she offered, which was thought-provoking.

There is a certain type of man who will not forgive anyone more skilled than himself in any way, no matter how small.

"May well turn yer stomachs," Redfist muttered. Janaire ladled her own three-quarter bowl and our red barbarian a double-measure; Diyan clattered back with a handful of picks. *He* received a double-measure as well, and Gavrin his usual ladle-and-a-half. Then Atyarik, and she only gave Ninefinger a single dollop. When she had settled with her own bowl, I poured wine, conspicuously not filling the blond giant's glass.

Perhaps he would ignore the subtle hint, too. Or perhaps I wished to provoke him. He didn't wait for everyone to be served, his left paw almost dwarfing his bowl and his picks tapped once against the table to make them the same length. He slurped at the *qu'anart*, making a face as if it offended him.

"Well." I returned to my seat, and Darik reached for a piece of bread. "It appears someone wants our beloved red-haired giant dead."

Gavrin stared at me for a long moment or two, glanced at Redfist, then bent over his bowl. Diyan had settled on my left side, dragging his heavy wooden chair forward with some difficulty. I tore a chunk of bread in half and handed it to the boy. The Antai do not make sponge, their long loaves are pillowy with crisp crusts. It is an acquired taste, even when the crumb is not full of sawdust. I had my own eating-picks, tucked in my belt as every sellsword learns to do on her first campaign.

"Why?" Janaire sounded honestly perplexed, a line between her eyebrows. "Who could possibly want to harm you?" Her cheeks glowed from the exertion of cooking, and she tapped her picks once on the side of her bowl, to bring luck to the table.

Redfist coughed, slightly, and he turned almost as red as Gavrin's throat. Watching the two of them blush like boys when a true *adai* spoke to them was only amusing the first few times. "Ah. Well. You see..."

"Did you think he was naught but a mere sellsword?" Ninefinger could barely contain himself. "This is the chosen Connaiot Crae ye speak to, ye *tannocks*."

"Means less than nothing to them, Corran." The ruddy giant dabbed at his bowl with an eating-pick, squinting as if he saw a future in the silky-textured fish stew. "Means even less than *that* in Skaialan, now."

"Only because you will nae return." Corran's tone took on something close to wheedling. This sounded an old argument, one rehearsed more than twice. "I tell you, Dunkast and his Black Brothers will ruin us all, Standing

Stones to the devil's arse, and we look for our Connaiot Crae to help us."

"My own sworn kin put me in chains." Redfist shook his head. "I'll hear no more of this."

"Perhaps it would help if we had the tale from the beginning." I lifted my bowl with both hands, enjoying the heat for a few moments. There was a scrape across my knuckles from last night's games, as well. "Then we could decide—"

"The men are speaking, *ban'sidha prutaugh*," Corran's wounded face wrinkled itself together as he wielded his picks, bringing a chunk of whitefish to his slavering mouth. The Skaialan words sounded *highly* uncomplimentary, but I knew little of that tongue then.

"Mind yerself, laddie." Redfist placed his eating picks carefully across his bowl. He had grown quite adept with them; I gathered in his homeland they ate with other implements. Which sparked a thought, and I eyed Corran afresh. "That's Kaia Steelflower ye're addressing."

"Is tha'it? Ye've been dragged after the smell of an elvish cunt?"

A thick silence fell. Even Gavrin ceased his single-minded absorption of food and stared, his mouth slightly open. His uneasy Pesh complexion had cleared marvelously over our sea-voyage; adventure seemed to suit him.

Ninefinger's sneer deepened, his oiled mustache drooping into his beard. "Rainak Redfist, dragged about by a little brown hoor. You, elvish bint, does he shag you from one end and your *shulleigh* there from the other? Is that how tis?"

I hate that word. I regarded Corran evenly, my left thumb running along a chip on the side of the bowl, a snag in its worn-smooth lacquer. There is something to be said for simply letting a man turn his own tent into a privy.

"Kaia?" D'ri's pleasant expression matched his tone, but he spoke in G'mai, and the inflection was perhaps unconsciously royal—a *s'tarei* formally addressing his *adai*. "Has the large foul one offered you insult?"

"He may think so." I prepared my picks, the hot bowl cradled in my left hand. "I remain unconvinced."

"So I may not chastise him?" His pleasant tone frayed very slightly. If he was playing the belling hound, I would play the silent one, and though the others did not understand my native tongue, the tone was probably clear enough.

Redfist's right hand turned into a fist the size of a small club. Even if he considered me well able to answer any insult in my own manner, he had some measure of standing to lose in the gaze of the rest of our small troupe.

"Not during dinner." I smiled, the bright unsettling expression I sometimes used over dice. I had not played since Hain, there being no time. Now, of course, I could not be certain I would not witch them to roll a certain way, and that is a dangerous pastime indeed.

"May I?" Atyarik had not yet touched his food, either. His intonation was slightly different, but clearly that of a *s'tarei* who had seen a wrong arise, and would have liked to right it.

Strange. He disliked me, or at least gave a good impression of it. To see him ruffle his plumage when a female sellsword was called a featherseller was intriguing. G'mai has no word for those who heal with the body or sell its pleasures to survive, but travel does have a way of broadening one's vocabulary.

"Corran." Redfist laid his left hand on his friend's shoulder, and his whole arm turned to stone. His blunt fingers curved, crushing, and there was a slight creaking. "Kaia Steelflower is *wal'kir*, and you are offering insult."

Sweat stood out on Corran's mushroom-pale brow. "*Wal'kir*? That piece of harbor shite?" He spat something else in Skaialan, too, and I did not need a translation to tell what he thought of a woman half his size who could still break his nose and accuse him of treachery. Of course, an innocent man might have taken more offense at the latter than the former, and whatever else Corran Ninefinger was, I would gamble my boots *and* my *dotani* that "innocent" did not apply no matter which language you pronounced it in.

Redfist surged up, bumping the table with a nasty, solid sound. Corran was flung backward, his chair breaking with the crack of well-seasoned wood, and Redfist—disturbingly fast for his size—pivoted, his massive boot lashing out and catching Corran's middle almost before the other giant hit the flagstones. The wall shuddered as Corran hit, and Redfist was on him again in a moment, hauling him up by his heavy green woolen tunic. Cloth tore, and Redfist roared, slamming him again into the shoulder-high stone wainscoting, the wood above it popping a long pale sliver.

Atyarik's hand settled on Janaire's wrist; she retreated into her own chair slowly, glancing at me with the huge eyes of a frightened doe. Diyan whistled, a long low tone of wonder, and Gavrin slid down in his seat as if he had been at too much mead. His eyes were round as well, and he had gone chalky under his Pesh coloring.

I sipped at my *qu'anart*. Very good, smooth as Hain fire-gossamer. "Besides," I said, when Redfist's roar had died, "it seems—" *Thud, thwack,* "—our friend Redfist—" *Crash, crack, grunt,* "—is giving his fellow barbarian instruction on table etiquette."

Redfist surged for the hallway, taking his bleeding cargo with him.

Janaire's shoulders quivered, and her braids trembled too. "How can you be so *calm?*" Atyarik's fingers stroked her wrist, a soothing motion.

D'ri shook his head slightly. "He invited this man into my *adai*'s house."

135

That was an answer she could understand, at least. G'mai codes offer much protection to a guest, and to a guest of one's guests, but there were...limits...to the latter.

The noise drew down the hall, heading for the front door. I laid my bowl down, dabbed at my lips with my fingertips, and rose.

"Kaia?" D'ri, very quietly.

"'Tis dusk." My braids were heavy again, my neck aching. "Corran Ninefinger the clans may murder, and collect a fine load of tradewire or coin upon. But Rainak Redfist is my friend, and *him* they may not have." I ambled for the doorway, to watch over our barbarian as he beat his fellow giant out through the smallgate and into the street. He yelled something in Skaialan after him, and stamped past me back into the house.

I took the opportunity to study the street. One or two carters at the gates of other residences, a small load of *tanju* upon a two-wheeled shaw-sled accompanied by a squatting bare-chested youth, poised to take advantage of the Antai custom of craving small tart fruit after dinner, and lengthening shadows on the tiled roofs.

My throat had dried, and my pulse turned to cantering hoofbeats in my ears and wrists.

So. Tonight, then.

I followed Redfist into the villa, and barred the smallgate.

SAFER IF I WERE NOT

THE KITCHEN, WITH ITS STONE ceiling and ancient, balky oven, was warm enough to draw sweat. Already Janaire had scoured every surface and taken inventory of pots and plate, and the faint scent of disuse that filled other corners of the villa was absent.

Redfist hissed a little as Janaire dabbed at his bleeding knuckles. "Corran is nae a bad sort," he said. "Fresh from the highlands, is all. Safest elsewhere."

"Not necessarily." I leaned against the wall next to the locked-and-barred door, near the iron bulk of the still-hot oven, moving my *dotani* to a slightly more comfortable angle upon my back. "*When hunting a wolf, first bloody the deer.*"

"Not familiar—ssss! Not familiar with that one, K'ai." He kept his hands on the long, thick wooden cooktable, squinting in place of flinching every once in a while.

I would have been surprised if he *had* been, since I'd spoken in G'mai. "If you hang out a piece of meat, soon the dogs will be along." It didn't have quite the same ring in tradetongue.

"Are ye meaning—" His eyebrows drew together, and his blue glance was sharp. His native tongue was rubbing through his words, much as I suspected G'mai cropped up through mine lately.

"I mean a watch could be set for Skaialan giants not leaving Antai, but returning." I did not lift my fingers to tick the points off, but I was sore tempted to. "Or this Ninefinger could have brought a commission, and as soon as he located you all he has to do is bring you to a certain place, at a certain time. Perhaps the commission was even meant to include him and sealed, in the way of such things, so any loose thread could be knotted away as well." How could he not see as much?

Then again, there is no one as adept at scenting—and building—treachery as an assassin. I had cause to be wary, after...

After Rikyat.

Redfist shifted on the clunky three-legged stool, wood creaking under his bulk. "He just *arrived*, how could—"

"Why does he handle eating-picks so easily? You are better at it now, but he did not eat with his full-ten fingers as you still did in Hain, now did he." It was not a question.

Redfist stared at his hand. The swelling was easing, Janaire's soft dabbing with crushed woundheal paste not nearly as efficacious as the Power she bound into the skin, swift tiny stitch-glyphs encouraging renewal. He swore, softly, and she glanced up in apology, one of her braids drooping a little loosely over her temple. They made a strange picture, the *adai* and the barbarian, her light grace and flowing dark green dress next to his mountainous shoulders and rough leather jerkin.

"'Tis a *guram* thing," he finally said, heavily, "to think of a kinsman."

Impatience skittered under my skin; I forced it away. "Is this Dun-kiest a kinsman as well?"

"In a manner of speaking."

My ears caught movement beyond the propped-open door, and my hand readied itself to leap for *dotani*-hilt. It was only Atyarik, melding out of the shadows with a *s'tarei*'s ease. His face was even longer than usual, his cheekbones painfully high because his mouth was pulled into the dourest frown I had seen on him yet. "We shall watch tonight," he informed me, in very formal G'mai. "Should the large rude one return, may I chastise him?"

I am glad you ask. If the Tyaanismir took a mind to quicken his draw, interesting times were ahead. "He was beaten bloody and tossed into the street, perhaps that is enough."

"He insulted the *adai* of the Heir of the Dragon Throne."

"We are a very long way from home, Tyaanismir-*sa*." *Or from that mattering.* The single syllable of the honorific was all the thanks I could offer him. After all, he was merely conscious of Darik's honor, not mine. "If he returns, wake me. No matter the hour."

He nodded, stiffly. Perhaps he thought a return of drunken or furious Corran Ninefinger was likely. I had other suspicions, but we would see. He glanced at Janaire, who nodded slightly, agreeing with him as an *adai* should. Her small shy smile was a wonder, erasing worry from her childlike face. The small fire in the great hearth snapped, adding to the heat, and I forced myself to think it through again. Piece by piece, in small bites, chewing thoroughly to avoid a surprise.

If I were after Redfist, and he had another of the Guild living in his house, it would be a waiting game. Unless the commission was large enough, in which case many shadows could slip into the house to overwhelm any resistance. I needed to know more.

"Redfist." Tradetongue slipped in my mouth, became harsher than I intended. "I need to know what ill this Dunkiest bears you, so I know what he might pay to have you eliminated."

"Does it matter?" Redfist flexed his fingers. "My thanks, Jenaih. It feels much better."

139

"Tis my pleasure." She tidied her healer's implements—a bowl of water, the woundheal paste, more dried woundheal and a dollop-glass of mead to soak pinches of the pungent herb in, the rust-streaked grindstone to crush-mix it. It stops the woundrot best if you use a ruststone, and she had applied quite a bit, since *baia* was out of season.

She might even try to bandage Redfist, but I did not think him likely to let her wrap him like a dumpling.

"You are marvelous healer, Gavridar." I searched for an appropriate compliment. "Any Temple of the Moon would be glad of your skill."

Did she flinch? Why? I had said it as gently as I could.

"Better healer than a teacher." She swept everything together and hurried from the room, leaving the flask of mead on the cook-table to slosh dangerously as Redfist shifted his weight. Atyarik turned sharply, pacing after her.

Even when I praised, she took it like a knife. "The fault is your student, not you," I called after her, but I could not be certain she heard. Her tender feelings were not the pressing issue, though. I forced myself to think in tradetongue again. "It matters, friend Redfist. It may be the difference whether one or two assassins are sent, or many more."

"What more does he want? I *left*." Redfist's sides heaved with a gusty sigh; he gazed at the mead bottle as if it held the answer. No doubt it held temptation, but an answer is another matter entirely. "A coward's move, that."

"Begin at the beginning," I prompted. "We may be interrupted at any moment; I would like to know why I am about to kill on your behalf."

"Ye do nae have to." A stubborn jut to his red-furred jaw, his coppery eyebrows drawing together with thunderous displeasure.

"You are my *friend*, Redfist."

"Might be safer if I were not."

There it was, again. Did Redfist think I would leave *him* to die on a battlefield, too? I forced my jaw to loosen, took a deep breath. "Nevertheless."

"Very well." He lifted the small mead-bottle, took a healthy dose, and set it down half empty. "Dunkast will never sit easy as a chieftain until I am dead."

"Chieftain of your clan?" Well, I supposed, many had been killed for less.

He muttered a few Skaialan words I was fairly sure were obscenities, and still gazed longingly at the mead bottle. "Not precisely. Each man has a clan, and a chieftain. There are no kings in the North, but there is the Connaiot Crae, and our last was my father." He studied his bruised hands, the consonants of tradetongue growing harsher and the vowels more lilting, the shape of another language thrusting through the argot like rocks through thin topsoil. "My very own father, and Dunkast's too. The Ferulaine is a bastard son, and won his following by battle, not blood. Though some said twas treachery that paved his way, and the blackest of sorcery. As long as I live, Dunkast cannot claim the Connaiot Crae. Tis only when my head is mounted on the wall of Belcarock, or another keep, that he will be the Crae. They will have no choice."

"Is this cu-roigh an inheritance?"

"If the Crae has a son blooded in battle the clans will follow. Especially if they respect him." His red-furred chin sank to his capacious chest. His jerkin, freshly brushed, was dark with use and wear, butter-soft. "There were many who would have followed me, even when those opposed to Dunkast began having...accidents. It matters little now; they will nae follow a *sunbrollaugh*."

"What is that?"

"A father-killer." Redfist had gone pale. "Such a man cannot be the Crae, and I would have called Dunkast to the rounds for the accusal. Except he had me clapped in irons. Me, his own kin."

"Did—"

"Of course not!" His wounded hands closed, viciously, as if he felt a neck to snap between them. "But Dunkast had his lying Black Brothers to swear suspicion on me, enough so that his craven arselickers could say twas legal."

That was not what I wished to ask. Still, I could not fault him for leaping at the question. "You said Dunkast killed your father."

His mouth turned grim, pulling against itself. "I feel in m'gut that he did, but I cannot, for the life of me, tell *how*."

"So, this leadership of the highlands—"

"Tis not so simple. The Crae leads us to war, and dispenses justice when clans cannot agree. My father was the head of the Redfist, and he was the Crae by acclamation. He said there was more to be gained from trade than raiding, and there were those who chafed at it. Dunkast was one. Then there was the battle against the blue hillfolk at Skarmout, and my bastard brother came back...changed."

Blue hillfolk? Is that like red-eyed bugger? A ticking silence filled the kitchen, from the oven's cooling skin and the chilly night-breath from the harbor walking up the hills. "Changed?"

The barbarian's gaze had turned faraway, pupils swelling a little as the candle on the table danced and the fire sank low into its banking. His words lilted further. "You and your kind may know of witchery, K'ai. But what lives past Skarmout, in the caves...that you do nae know of, and should be glad. Dunkast was once my brother, one I didnae much like but still loved. When he came back from that battle, something else was inside him."

A chill finger traced up my back. What traveling sellsword hasn't heard whispers of such things, or seen wonders? The world is wide, and strange Powers fill every inch of it. There was the bird-witch outside Vulfentown, and the whispering coven of Imr-Amjal with their cloying incense and fish-scale tattoos, drugged windwitches on the Shelt and the cannibal monsters the Kmeri claim stalk the forest-shore at the other edge of their grassy sea. Holysingers who may walk unscathed through a furnace, goddesses speaking through their blindly ecstatic followers during festivals, the sun standing still as the last of the Pensari called his curse down upon the slums and dregs...yes, *something* living in the northern highlands giants inhabited was not very hard to believe.

"Whatever witchery he has matters little," I said, finally. "You have Kaia Steelflower at your back, Redfist."

He nodded, and the silence returned.

There was no more to be said. At least, not so far as I was concerned. Yet I could not tell if he thought my aid a comfort—or another danger to be navigated.

ROOF DANCING

PERHAPS THEY THOUGHT TO CATCH me sleeping, though I would be the only one in the house familiar with their ways. But kafi is more than simply a pleasure; it is like chai—it warms one and props the eyelids up, for a short while at least. Tucked against a chimney, I avoided the worst of the wind, and as the kitchen fire settled further into its banked sleep the warm stone cooled by degrees. It reminded me of other chilly nights in Antai, spent watching rooftops or a single candlelit window, moving just enough to keep the blood from cramp-condensing in legs and arms.

At intervals—sometimes shorter, sometimes longer—a shadow flitted over one edge of the rooftop or another, or drifted past in the street. D'ri or Atyarik, swimming silent as fish in dark water. Any assassin worth the name would look for the silent knife to match their pacing, but the kitchen chimney was a fool's place to linger. For one thing, it left the entire front of the house out of sight.

Even the great masters of the Guild, however, would underestimate a *s'tarei*. Or an *adai* who could thin the walls between her mind and the great cacophony of others thinking, breathing, and feeling to sense fierce determination or cold expectance. Shivers ran down my back, muscles gripping in waves as I held myself grimly to the task. The *taih'adai* could teach me the basics of controlling Power, but practice was the only way to achieve any *mastery*. There were still the final starmetal spheres to endure, but Janaire had said nothing of them since we made landfall.

Many thoughts kept me company that long night. I could not fend off every assassin in the city, for one. For another, now that Ninefinger had been beaten into the street, he was in no little danger. I did not care overmuch, but I had not been able to question him. He might have been able to shed some light on the exact dimensions of the purse sent to buy Redfist's death, and once I knew those borders, I would be able to decide how to make leaving the giant alone a more attractive proposition.

The added benefit of interrogating the blond barbarian and possibly making his clan-name Eightfingers, or Five, was not to be dismissed, either.

I also wondered what Redfist thought, his pallet in the cellar less comfortable than his room but certainly more secure. Puff-poison could be breathed through a reed under the door, but between Janaire's healing and my admittedly imperfect knowledge of the toxins each throat-cutting clan liked to use, he stood a good chance of surviving even that. *Hala*, that black death, was expensive, and it was unlikely they would use it this early in the game.

For such it is, when a thief or assassin sets herself to guard a precious thing, instead of taking it. That the stakes are higher than *banhua* does not make it less a board with rules to bend or flout to win.

You must know the pattern before you may change the dance.

My attention constricted, pinpointing an inky, dangerous dart approaching the villa. I did not tense, my breathing did not alter, but my pulse rose slightly, my eyelids fluttering.

D'ri. The *taran'adai* bloomed inside me, a secret, almost-painful flower, a whisper blending with the wind. *'Ware, they come.* I hoped it was his watch, and I was not waking him. The south wall held two blots, their quick feet avoiding sharp glassine shards set in mortar along the top to dissuade climbers less graceful or lucky; I located two more at one end of the street, loping easily for our villa. Last but not least, an almost-invisible shape blurred along the roofline, and if not for Janaire's teaching I would have had only uneasy instinct to warn me.

Travel-boots were no use and I had no glove-shoes, so it had taken me a half-candlemark to fashion felted strips, wrapped just tightly enough and tied in a particular manner over the instep, up the ankle as well. In winter, the Danhai wrap their feet thus before thrusting them into their boots, and it was a highly prized skill among both the army and the irregulars.

You have to kill enough of them to study the wrappings, of course.

I blurred silently along, bent double and parallel to the roofline, and felt D'ri's answering warmth. No time for speaking, even in the *taran'adai'*s quickness, for I was already unfolding to catch the roof-runner—perhaps a lookout, or perhaps the main assassin, who could tell just yet—from behind. Roof-tiles shifted, slight betraying noises, and he had half-turned before I was on him, blackened knife sinking into the kidney with disconcerting milk-clot ease. Twisting, wrenching it free, my other hand cupping a muffled chin and yanking it aside, force transferred as his knees buckled and my mouth full of sourness. Hit with a clatter, breath forced from my lungs and the entire world wheeling, knife free and dragged across his throat, my legs snakelike around his waist as if we were lovers. Hot spray of blood pattering the damp tiles, he turned to deadweight and I *pushed.* Now I had to get free before he carried me over the edge—a crushing blow on my knee, my breath sucking in hard and harsh, kicking the small of his back and my fingernails splitting as I clawed at tiles, shedding momentum.

Eyes closed, a red mist rising behind my lids as a low deadly whistle clove the air. D'ri, night-hunting. A soft, choked gurgle from the south wall—Atyarik, perhaps? Two *s'tarei*, one with a bow, could wreak deadly havoc on invaders. As long as I kept the roof clear—

Hit me *hard*, driving me up the slope and knocking my breath free for a single gasp-lunging moment. I had thrown myself into a crouch, so she did not manage to plunge her own black blade into my gut; something metal went skitter-chiming away. A breath of sickening *annua* smell—dear gods, the root would make her unholy fast, and now I knew it was female, because her labored breathing passed through a throat my size. I twisted her wrist, heard a crackle as bones ground together in my grasp, and threw my head back, hitting the bridge of her nose with the much-harder curve of my own skull. Padded by my braids and the masking fabric over her mouth, it was nonetheless a painful blow, and no doubt she saw pain-constellations whirling in a brief spangling dark.

Lunging for my feet, fabric slipping and toes splaying, one of my toenails tearing with a brief hot pain, whirling to get my arm up as she stamped, *hard*, her glove-boots much better than mine and the inner edges decked with sharpwire. A clatter of greatbow pulleys, carrying in the chill damp air, and a dull splat a good threepace from me, a bubbling, evil green smell spreading. I inhaled, pitching aside again as her foot flicked—Mother's *tits* but she was fast—and the spread of the *dolquieua* oil higher on the slope would force me down unless I could get past it.

The thought of landing on the wall—or the courtyard's flags and stone benches—brought me up and just as quickly down again, rolling past the greenish splotch. Calculating trajectory, likely angles—I ran

147

crabwise up the slope, hoping the shifting shadows would throw off the bowman's aim. More clatters and soft cries from below, stinging in my eyes—D'ri's sweat, and my own. I had retained my own knife, thank the Moon, and dodged again instinctively. I *felt* the arrow pass, with an iron head instead of a friable poison-carrying one, and it plowed up a spray of tile-chips that stung as I dove through them, landing on my back with my left foot flicking up to help the female assassin on her leap. She had meant to close with me again, but I had vanished, and now my toes sank into her midriff. Had I been wearing boots I could have perhaps ruptured something instead of merely deflecting her a few critical degrees. She hit with a snap and a crunch, and I drew in my knees, then flung my feet out and was upright with a gut-tearing effort. Another thunking sound, and I threw myself backward. We were moving too quickly, or perhaps luck was with me, for *that* arrow—another slow, poison-freighted, fragile bulb at its tip—smacked into my opponent.

Who let out the only scream of the roof-games, a high stuttering cry as the *dolquieua* chewed through fabric and flesh. It cannot puncture tile, and water will wash it into irrelevance, but in its first few moments in the open air after an impact, the "eating moss" is awful indeed.

Kaia? D'ri, a flood of concern almost knocking me from my perch. I shelved it, sliding now, both feet out, slamming into the body with a jolt that robbed me of momentum. It tumbled, loose-jointed and still screaming, at the angle that would send it down into the courtyard.

If she survived the fall, and survived the poison for a little while, I would question her. At the moment I was horribly exposed on the long incline, temporarily at a standstill, and there was an archer who had this part of the roof under the arc. Another effort, a small sound escaping me as I heaved myself aside, one of my knives jammed back in its sheath and my hand flicking up to catch my *dotani*'s hilt.

The metal would glimmer, and throw off the archer's aim.

I plunged over the ridgebeam, the pulley clatter and twang of another bowstring releasing roughening my back with cold fearsweat. Dropping down and sliding, right foot snapping out to break the knee of the third roofrunner, probably the most experienced of the lot and almost invisible. For a moment I did not know why I had kicked, and my *dotani* sang a low note of air-cleaving. A solid *tchuk*, carving the fingers off this wiry deathbringer's right hand, and to do him credit, he did not scream, not even when I tumbled him down into the ragged, winter-ready garden and Atyarik's cruelly efficient blade. I finished on hands and knees, my sides heaving and my stomach a ball of roiling, and my *dotani* slid back into its home with reflexive, habitual speed.

That was when the screaming began, so I did the only thing I could, tile-edges scraping my palms as I caught the edge of the roof, feetfirst through the deliberately unlatched shutter to Redfist's room. I expected to shatter glass, but at least one assassin had taken the invitation, and the noise within was Janaire's voice, high and terrified, breaking on a choking gasp.

"*Kaia he has a knife*—" She clutched at her left arm as if it pained her, staggering into the wall next to the fireplace, the assassin howling as Power-fueled flames crawled over his clothing. Steaming smoke gouted, a sickeningly appetizing smell of roasting filled the room as this assassin beat ineffectually at the twisting, hissing tongues. A small shape in the corner—dark hair, too tiny to be an assassin or—

I ducked the flaming man's blind lunge, weight dropping into my back leg and the other flicking up and out, sinking into his stomach again. He promptly folded in half and began to vomit, water and other matter spewing from nose and mouth. *"Douse the fire!"* I yelled in G'mai, and to her credit, even with her wounded arm she had the presence of mind to obey.

Smoke filled my nose, stung my eyes, I had the measure of the half-charred assassin now and tapped him behind the knee. He went down hard; it was a moment's work to immobilize him and snap, "Cloth, rope, something! Something to tie him up with!"

Janaire leaned against the wall, deathly pale, her braids askew. She was still dressed—what in the name of the gods was she doing in here?

The moan from the corner froze me in place, and it was a good thing the burnt assassin was only semiconscious.

For the small, wrongly-twisted shape in the corner was Diyan.

ANSWERS TO GIVE

"I TOLD YOU. I TOLD you *both*." I tossed Atyarik a roll of bandaging-cloth, and examined Diyan's side again, rolling him slightly aside on the small table that had survived the melee in Redfist's room. Already the bruising had begun, flesh suffusing with blood in protest. The cut was ill-looking, but the boy was not gutsplit, thank the Moon and every foreign god. It looked painful. "Bar your door, stay there, do *not* come out unless your window is breached, I said as much!"

The boy's breathing was shallow and hollow, and his eyelids fluttered. I cursed in Shainakh, in Pesh, and to finish it off, wished ill on the assassin's mother in rolling shipboard slang. Steadied my hands and sponged the blood away, carefully, wincing as the little one inhaled sharply. The broiled assassin was a lump on the floor, bound hand and foot and retreating into unconsciousness.

He had to know what awaited him was likely to be painful, too.

"He heard a noise." A few dots of blood stippled Janaire's flawless cheek, and her braids were mussed. She winced as Atyarik tested her arm. Probably broken, and it served her right. "I said not to...*ssss*, Mother Moon have mercy..." She sounded very, very young. "I said not to, but he unbolted the door."

"Stupid little farrat." The G'mai words escaped my mouth whole, with a tender inflection that hurt my throat. No discoloration at the edges of the wound. Just the blood, and that horrific bruising. "*Cha*, little one, be still." I slapped his hand down and away as he feebly struck out. The Vulfentown slang sat uneasily on my tongue. Dare I send for a Temple healer? Janaire could tend her own gods-be-damned arm; I gathered the boy's weight in my arms and heaved. He was so limp, and had put on more weight—now, I could barely haul him from the table. Carrying him through the streets—I could hail a legwheel, perhaps?

My frustration spiked, my hands gluing themselves to Diyan's side as the boy flailed, perhaps in response to the pain of being touched. One slackened fist clipped the bridge of my nose with uncoordinated, impossible-to-divert speed, and the blow flung my head back. Now *I* was the one seeing constellation-patterns behind my lids, and a torrent of foul language spilled from my mouth, my hands *burning*, burning as if thrust into a well-made fire. Fingers cramped, bearing down, the darkness beating over my sight with soft downy wings.

Slice, flesh parting along the blade, and the small body's training made him drop away from the cold touch of steel. Perhaps it saved his life, but the blow came from nowhere, a kick right on the wound, tearing and clotting and bruising and the pain all through him, could not   breathe   could   not   breathe   notbreathe notbreatheNOTBREATHE—

I spilled to the floor, lungs laboring fruitlessly, a gigantic cramp seizing my left side. The damage ran deeper than I had suspected, and everything blackened, a faint sense of motion and noise far away.

CRACK. A massive impact smashed into me, and I surfaced with a jolt, my side aching and heat roaring through my wounded cheek. Atyarik, his lean fist knotted in my jerkin, nodded, and dropped me next to a still-steaming, motionless almost-corpse.

The *s'tarei* had slapped me, to shock me back into myself.

Janaire's soft weeping mixed with Diyan's sobs. The boy all but wailed, and Janaire sought to hold him with her good arm, seeking to comfort. Atyarik felt at her arm again, and I closed my eyes, heart and lungs functioning again, everything else protesting in the strongest possible terms. I had not filled my trousers, though, as some do when death brushes past.

A sellsword is grateful for such things.

I pushed myself up, shakily, on hands and knees.

"This will hurt," Atyarik said, very softly, in G'mai. His *adai* did not flinch.

"Do it." The words broke on a sob, and he made a swift, violent motion to seat the bone in its proper space. Power rasped and slid against the parts of me still raw from the healing, and my forehead hit wooden floorboards. My small piping cry was lost in the larger noise, Janaire's scream swallowed halfway and Diyan's frightened howl bespeaking an ecstasy of fear.

I did not blame him.

The wood was cold, and felt good against my fevered palms and forehead. I uncurled, slowly, cautiously. Other than an angry ache in my side and the nips and aches of roofside combat mouthing my limbs, I was well enough. My face hurt, and I would no doubt look like a painted Rijiin courtesan in a little while.

A cricket-buzz, something tickling inside my head. Darik's voice, very small. *Kaia?*

Are there more? Pushing the words through the icy fog surrounding me was difficult, and the ringing left in their wake was disconcerting. I shuddered, forced myself to stillness. It had not been this difficult to reach him before, but then again, we had not tried to communicate through walls.

Or had we? I could not remember just at the moment.

A fuzzy sense of worry, strained through multiple layers of cloth like *altan* dye. *None. For now.*

Keep watch. It was unfair to place the burden upon him, but at the moment I could not move.

It took a short while before I could. When I straightened, wincing at the hot metal buried in my side, I saw Diyan on the table, his upper half resting against Janaire, who steadied him with her unbroken right arm. Atyarik had his hand clamped around the break on her left—high up, the large bone in the upper part of the limb—and was sweating, as well. A sheen stood out on Janaire's forehead; she stared up at her *s'tarei*, trust and open hope stamped on her soft riverland features.

She could have died, had she not had the presence of mind to light the last assassin on fire.

Diyan's big dark eyes shone with tears. He in turn gazed adoringly up at the Gavridar lowlander, snot bubbling on his upper lip, and he perhaps thought *she* had healed him. Well enough.

"Move them." My tone was a harsh croak. "Down to the cellar, with Redfist. Guard them."

Atyarik nodded. Janaire shut her eyes, Power feathering lightly over her arm, sinking in. With Atyarik to steady her, she could perform a deeper healing and be well in a few days, the bone mended seamlessly.

I watched him half-carry Janaire, Diyan leaning against her other side as if he had been at mead, and did not move to help. Followed the sounds of them moving through the house with my eyes closed, my entire body a taut string, and heard other creaks and stealthy movement, too clumsy to be one of the Guild or the clans.

When I opened my eyes, Gavrin peered at me from the half-open door. I exhaled sharply.

How was I to protect them if they would not *listen?*

"I heard..." He was deathly pale. "Kaia..."

"Go back to your room, or come in and help me." I took stock of my weapons, my feet, my aching muscles. I would have to hope more dancers would not arrive for a short while.

I bent to the steaming ruin on the floor, told my back it was simply going to have to accept the punishment I was about to deal both it and the rest of me, and began to think about how I could prop this lucky assassin in a chair.

Before he died, he had answers to give.

No Songs of This

I AM NOT AN ARTIST of pain. But I survived two winters of the Danhai campaign, and when my home is invaded and those under my protection wounded, I am willing to match anything I saw in those icy or broiling but always violent seasons. Gavrin vomited once, when I cut the man's jerkin and shirt free and the full extent of the burns became visible. Even in the low firelight, the lacerated, steaming meat was enough to unseat any stomach's cargo.

Fortunately—I suppose—once the man regained consciousness and began moaning, the burns were worth more than any amount of additional havoc I could wreak on his physical frame. He told me, between gasps and pleadings, everything I needed to know, and when I was certain there was no more, I applied pressure on both sides of the large pulse in his neck until he was unconscious again, then slit his throat. It was a measure of mercy; the burns were fatal, and their murder of him would be far more protracted and painful.

He bled out in moments, the hot spray splashing my face and hands, just as the tide shifted. Tower bells along the perimeter of the harbor sounded, marking the change. Many ships would be leaving soon, most braving only the western coast of the Lan'ai. It was late to be sailing across the Shelt, but there was still profit to be made until the ice-wind began to blow and it was time to do naught but scrape hulls and repair nets.

Tis the giant we want, and fat is the reward.

I sagged against the small table, covered in blood, my knees suspiciously watery. I had to *think*, but my head was full of a strange buzzing. Gavrin, still pale, wiped at his mouth with the back of his hand again, nervously. He kept glancing at me as if he expected to be next. No doubt the scene would offend Janaire's tender mercies as well.

Think. There are things to do next. You must do them, nobody else can. My lips moved, soundlessly, and I hoped the blood did not carry disease. It was a strange worry, one I had never felt before, but it loomed larger and larger until blessed silence filled my head. It was a relief, that quiet, and I did not care so much that it would shut the other G'mai out, including Darik. What mattered was I had some space, some calm.

First, there was the blood to deal with, and the corpses. Then there was enough of Ammerdahl Rikyat's bloody Shainakh gold to travel, and everything in the trunk the Head had been holding for me to be packed afresh.

Then, there was leaving Antai. I could not think of a direction likely to give us much in the way of comfort, but outside the city, I could be fairly certain of Redfist's safety. At least, as far as the Guild was concerned. The commission did not extend past the walls.

That was the only piece of knowledge he had resisted giving me. A credit to the Guild, and perhaps there was another Sorche left to grieve him. He was old enough to have an apprentice or two.

"Gavrin." The word was harsh; I switched to a collage of Pesh and tradetongue to make certain he could understand. I meant to thank him for his presence, perhaps, but something else came out entirely. "Will you write songs of this?"

He shook his head, the low uncertain light gilding some threads of honey among the muddy strands. His big troutfish hands cupped his sharp elbows, and he hugged himself like a child.

"Good." My head fell back, my braids resting against the wall. "I am...sorry for it." *This is a sellsword's life. I left anything else behind long ago.* The words curdled, I shook them away. "Go down to the cellar. Tell them it is safe enough, for now."

He nodded. His face firmed, but for a moment I saw a glimpse of the child he must have been in Pesh. Young, attractive slaves are much prized...but also in certain kinds of danger, and no wonder he left his homeland when he was manumit.

Of course, what Pesh slave would admit to escape?

It took determination to pursue Gavrin's chosen course, with his instrument and his wits, such as they were. A minstrel would be useful wherever we went, but he could supplement the household's earnings here, and when spring came, he could split the remaining funds with the remaining G'mai and the little one, and go on his way. A winter's worth of shelter was what I could offer, and to do so, I would have to move quickly.

He moved uneasily for the door, and when he had reached it, I spoke again.

"You are a fine minstrel." I did not know what else to say. Perhaps he even understood, but he did not halt.

STRAWS IN
YOUR STORM

THE CORPSES WERE PILED OUTSIDE the gate as dawn reddened the east, a bloody sunrise swelling like my wounded face. Darik examined me for a long moment in the courtyard, looking almost as tired as I felt after the night's festival. The bow in his hands was not as elegant as a G'mai's restrained, deadly curve, but it had served him well. He did not ask needless questions or gainsay me.

I was grateful, but the warmth could not escape the invisible wall surrounding me.

"Bastard Dunkast," Redfist said, in the kitchen, looking at his hands. "Had I thought him capable of this, I'd never have set sail with ye."

I nodded. "I know." We gazed at each other for a long moment, and his large shoulders stiffened as if I had shouted. "You might as well tell me, Redfist." I had guessed, of course. I had traveled too long with the ruddy giant not to suspect.

Guessing or suspecting is not the same as hearing it aloud, though.

"I return to the highlands." His ginger-furred hands slowly curled onto themselves. "Dunkast will meet me in the rounds, to answer for everything. Crae or not, law or no, I'll nae stop until I have his head."

"Very well." I glanced at Darik, who held a cup of blessedly hot chai in both hands, his hair wildly disarranged and his cheeks still painted with heat from the night's efforts. There was a fresh knife-slash on his jerkin, and his weariness made my own that much more savage. Thankfully, the strike had only caught fabric, not the skin underneath. "D'ri..."

"Your battles are mine," he said, softly. "When do we start?"

I was almost sorry he could not feel my own deep, nervous relief. "Today. Now. There is little time, we must have horses and travel gear, and be outside the walls by dusk."

Redfist tapped the table twice, lightly, as if he wished to pound upon it. "I could go alone. I *should* go alone, seeing as how I've endangered every one of you."

"You could." I watched the steam rise from a fire-blackened kettle, Gavrin hunching over it and rubbing at his hands as if they pained him. "But you will not. I will at least see you to your homeland safely."

Janaire, her arm bent and bound to immobilize it while healing sank into the bone, shook her head, managing to express pain and mutiny in one slight motion. "You cannot be serious. You *cannot*."

"You will stay here," I repeated, in that same remote, flat tone that was all I had the endurance to voice. "In spring you will take the small one to G'maihallan, and foster him."

Atyarik studied me curiously. "He is no *s'tarei*," he said, finally, but spread his hands when Janaire darted him a scorching look.

"Nevertheless," D'ri said quietly, and Atyarik bowed his head. To his credit, he was loyal to my Dragaemir princeling.

Was there a story I did not know, between them? Now I had no time to find out.

"As soon as we are past the walls the assassins will cease their visits." I accepted another hot bowl of chai from Gavrin, whose hands shook slightly. "Wintering here is not so bad."

"Kaia, these are your people—" Redfist began. I took a sip of chai, glad of the warmth, and stared at him over the rim of my bowl. Gavrin kept ladling, and Janaire winced, awkwardly accepting hers. She was thinner than when we had met, and her cheeks had hollowed slightly. It did not make her any less beautiful, but she was no longer the girl she had been.

"Yes." I regarded him steadily. "But I left my homeland." *And you are my fellow sellsword.*

"I do not ask ye to come." He had paled, and was almost transparent. It was a change to see him so grave, and of all of us, he was the one left unwounded.

And the minstrel, of course. Gavrin's quiet was unnerving. Had he finally seen enough of sellswording to understand it was not to be poured into silly couplets?

"I know." I longed to shut my eyes, savor the chai, pretend.

"Your training is not finished." Janaire did not relent. "I am your *teacher*, Kaia. You could harm yourself—"

Not as much as I will harm others. "Yada'Adais." Very formally. "You have been kind to me, and I honor that. I am unworthy to be your student." I forged ahead, wishing I could climb the stairs and fall into the bed I would not be using this winter. "The last thing I will ask of you and your *s'tarei* is to keep our friend Redfist safe until I return with the horses."

Her chin lifted. "You do not care who you break, do you, Anjalismir Kaialitaa. We are all as straws in your storm."

It was meant to sting, especially in G'mai. I did not bother to tell her tales of straws buried in stone walls by a furious sky god's breath—I had seen such things, on the rim of the Danhai plains, once or twice. When the sky-dancers begin to whirl, any shelter is as dangerous as the open grass-sea itself.

My shoulders bowed under a fresh weight, and I accepted it as I would so much else that day. "Then it is best I am as far from those of different metal as possible, Yada'Adais." I set my chai-bowl down and left the kitchen on a tide of raised voices, Gavrin attempting to be heard over Atyarik, Janaire seeking to silence them both, and Redfist desperately seeking to restore some peace.

Any assassin who wandered in would probably be talked to death.

My head was already full of the next task I had to accomplish, and the next. D'ri followed me through the hall and up the stairs, and when we reached the dubious safety of my—*our*—room, I found myself forced to say something, anything, to break the purely physical silence. The *taran'adai* was a humming cord between us, full of the careful distance two people who do not agree can leave between themselves and a looming problem.

"You do not have to—" I began.

"Nor do you," he pointed out, catching my wrist. His fingers were warm, and gentle, and he gazed into my swollen face as if the discoloration and puffing did not bother him. "But you will, Kaialitaa, and I am your *s'tarei*."

"If you ask me to turn aside, to let him go..." My throat was too dry. "If you asked that of me, Darikaan, I would."

There. It was said. So much for the intangible I had carried to stiffen my back since I left Anjalismir's high white spires, the determination to chart my course alone. If I was the only flawed G'mai, then I would be worthy of such an insult from the gods themselves. A twisted manner of pride, a child's determination.

Who was I, now? Once that determination was taken away, who *was* Kaia Steelflower?

His hand softened, and instead of my wrist he held my hand, our fingers interlacing as if they had been shaped specifically to do so. Even our calluses matched. "How long would it be before you hated me, if I did?"

There is a word in G'mai for the dart that strikes the heart but does not kill. It is a small, sharp word, and it pains one even to hear it. I had never understood its full intricacy, the depth of its meaning, before. He lifted my hand, pressed his lips to my bruised, battered knuckles. I had not even washed tile-dust from my face or hands, and my braids were probably a rumpled mess. He did not seem to mind.

"I could not hate you." Who was the woman using my voice? She sounded almost as young as Janaire, and almost as soft.

"Even so. I shall find the horses. You may want a bath before we go." He hesitated, his breath warm against my stinging knuckles. Touched them again with his mouth, very softly, as if to ease a child's scrapes. "Redfist says the North is a cold place."

I should have told him he was weary as well, and might want a soaking as well. Instead, I stood like a statue, and he disappeared through the door before I could summon even the pretense of a protest. Was this what it meant to have a *s'tarei*, or was I simply becoming lazy?

I did not know.

CERTAIN PROPERTIES

IT BEGAN TO DRIZZLE, A chill dispirited prickle-rain Clau sailors call *moonbreath*, for they believe her the source of all cold, as the sun is all heat. I hunched, watching the paved expanse of the North Road from the shelter of a cranyon tree's bulk, its branches not yet naked but full of painted, dying leaves in their last vibrancy. Antai simmered in its cup, down to the liquid glitter of the harbor, smoke-haze frothing like the foam on well-whisked chai. The ponies— shaggy beasts with wise eyes and mischievous dispositions—were much smaller than any I would have selected. Redfist, however, pronounced them the best choice for the North in this season. There were no Skaialan drafts in the markets; the farmers in the hinterlands prizing them too highly to send them down into the bowl. Our giant was too big for the ponies, but his legs had carried him from Hain to a battlefield, then back to Vulfentown and over the sea. Once we were through the Pass, he said, he could find a mount if he wished.

He laughed when he said it, a bitterly amused snort, and I was too tired to ask why.

A little farther up the Road, well out of even crossbow range, a slatternly tavern leaned against its gray-weathered stable. No doubt it was crawling with fleas, but safe enough for Redfist to sit with a tankard for a short while.

A few hours along the North Road was the farthest I had gone in that particular direction from Antai.

Just as the Danhai plains were the farthest I'd gone from the Rim itself. I was too exhausted to suppress the shudder that always went through me when I dwelled too long on those two years.

Even through the chill, rising mist, I sensed the heat of approaching murder. I stepped away from the tree, my *dotani* ringing from its sheath. We were lucky the commission had not been high enough to interest a daykiller. *Those* are almost impossible to halt, and their price reflects as much.

No, this Dunkast perhaps did not understand Antai's Guild, or there was a reason he wished Redfist murdered in the dark. He had paid in pale Northern gold, not the good ruddy gloss of Shainakh Rams, or so the smoking, stinking, reeking wreck of an assassin had told me. The hand that had carried the gold and the sealed packet of instruction was none other than Corran Ninefinger's; the blond giant could have been simply a stupid catspaw. Soon enough they would hunt him down, too, if they had not already. Redfist did not say what had prompted the blond giant to come south.

Put your worries away, Kaia. They are not needed here.

I took my position in the middle of the North Road's flagged expanse. Later, mud would creep across the stones in slow rivers, and here above the bowl, away from the harbor's breath, it would freeze. A pale cloud puffed from my mouth, drops flashing through it, and the shadows moved on the other side of the crumbling arc of walls that had been witchery-strong in the Pensari's day and manned with archers and guards during the warlord years that followed.

It had been a long while since the great city had needed its shell upon the hilltops, though.

Dusky rainlight turned them into cloak-wrapped enigmas, kerchiefs over their mouths, hoods dripping with moisture over *dhabris*. Hands folded inside wide sleeves, three of the Guild eyed me. I returned the favor.

One of them would be a representative of the clan who had sent last night's courtiers. One would be sent directly from the Head and the Council, to make certain proprieties were observed. The third would be a witness from another clan, one most likely *not* allied with the first. No doubt I would have to pay double-dues next tithing-season—if I returned. Most commissions have a provision for interference, but *hopefully* it was not large enough to tempt anyone outside the walls with winter fast approaching.

We eyed each other, and I tensed, my *dotani* rising slightly. Scuffling sounds, high fast breathing, and movement behind them. Two shadows, with a third held awkwardly between them.

They held thiefcatchers, long wooden spars age-darkened and banded with iron. Each had a prong, like a *yueh* rune that had lost half a leg to battleground injury; the shorter half ended in a *hocta*-knot around the prisoner's neck, the spare loop snugged under the armpits. The longer was attached to the girdle, and walking inside that contraption was unsteady at best and bloody at worst.

They call it the Chastity, for the short spikes on the inside.

She was forced to her knees before the three senior Guild members, and a muffled curse told me who it was. A chill spread over me.

Even if I forgave Sorche Smahua's-kin, there was still this to face. In another place, she might have chosen a sellsword's path instead of a clan, or had it chosen for her. Even if the first assassin had taken it upon herself to avenge Sorche's thiefmother, the elder woman should have restrained her. Not only had she robbed the clan of the investment her little thiefling had represented, but the clumsiness of said little thiefling had warned me to be wary and perhaps cost the Smoke—or another clan—part of a fat commission.

It was not the potential death of a Guild member in good standing they would punish her for. It was the loss of profit. There are many temples in Antai, many gods from both the hinterlands and abroad, but the one who rules beneath, above, and throughout them all had been disobeyed, and would take due vengeance.

One of the elders moved forward. Pointed, and the two with the thiefcatcher forced Sorche to her knees. A murmur was probably the delivery of the sentence in old Pensari, and a long silence showed where *that* word, the one that was never uttered, fitted into its contours. The sibilants carried, and a breeze shook the cranyon tree's leaves. A rattle as some fell, the wet gleam of a blade.

"*Mother!*" Sorche cried, just before the most senior clanmember, the one in the middle, wrenched her head back. She might have fought, too, but the other two had her arms and the thiefcatchers were braced. A high spattering jet of arterial blood, and I did not look away.

Some are children their entire lives. Hot rancid fluid boiled in my throat. There was no chai that would wash away the taste.

They watched as I strode for the wall-line; I felt a burst of concern—D'ri, wedged in the cranyon tree's upper reaches with his bow, as I moved forward and into bow-range from the crumbling stone. My left hand moved for a pocket, and I halted just on the other side of the invisible boundary.

I held up the Shainakh red Ram, its shine visible even in this darkness. The Moon hid her face behind a passing cloud, and I flicked the gold off my fingers in the thieves' way, the metal describing a high spinning arc before a dark-gloved hand blurred out to catch it.

167

"For her pyre," I said, as clearly as I could, in tradespeak.

One nodded, a fractional dip of the muffled head. They could have thrown her body over the wall. This way, at least, her spirit would rise on the smoke and join her thiefmother's, in whatever afterworld the two of them might share.

I turned my back on them, but I did not sheathe my *dotani*. I walked, steadily, for the cranyon again, its bole a wet pillar and its outline blurring with moisture. The thin piercing rain had soaked into my braids; they were heavy once more, my neck throbbing with tension. My teeth ached as well—I forced myself to loosen my jaw, despite the risk of the bubble in my throat bursting. If it did, I decided, I would swallow it.

And that was how we left Antai.

To Be Continued

STEELFLOWER
GLOSSARY

A-thatch, thatch'n – Displeased, insulted, angered but not to the point of blows

Adai – Female G'mai

Adai'mi/sa – My adai/Lady Adai (honorific)

Adjii – Adjutant

Albestrkha – alabaster

Baia – pungent plant/herb; "poor man's woundheal"

Ban'sidha prutaugh – ill-tempered whore

Cha – (Pidgin.) Expletive, inquiry, agreement, spare syllable.

Chaabi – Clau stew

Dauq'adai – Seeker

Dhabri – head-covering, headwrap

Dolquieua – green rot, "the eating moss"

Dotanii – sword – long and slightly curved, slashing blades with oddly shaped hilts meeting the hand differently than other blades

Fallwater – shower

Farrat – A ferret-like creature, but more closely related to cat than weasel

Hath'ar lak – The sleep after a battle, also a gift from a kindly grandmother or a quiet death in bed surrounded by relatives

Kaahai – Bitch, female donkey, balky mare

Kair'la – The same verb for sweet syrup-crystals dissolving in water, with insanity tacked onto the end.

Navthen – a chemical inside a clay ball that produces a hot burst of flame when mixed with ortox that coats the outside.

Piri-splitter cut – sword technique

Qu'anart – smoked fish or mutton

Rheldakh – a Pesh bird-goddess, known to give succor to travelers

S'tarei – male G'mai

S'tarei'mi/sa – My s'tarei / Sir

Shaurauq'g'd'ia - a foul emission from the loins of a diseased demon

Skai'atair - unclean, foul, outcaste, the dregs of a poisoned bowl, as well as assassin

Stilette – a thin, sometimes flexible blade

Sunbrollaugh – patricide

T'adai assai – "It is done."

Taih'adai – "Starseed" a teaching sphere

Tamadine – a particular unit of soldiers

Tannocks – idiots

Taran'adai – Speak-within (telepathy)

Vavir – a drug made from the *vavir* weed

Yada'adai's'ina – Literally, "student teacher"

Yada'Adais – G'mai teacher

Zaradai – witchlight

Read on for a preview of...

STEELFLOWER
IN SNOW

THE ROAD REMAINED EASY ENOUGH, THOUGH it began to climb on the third day. Slowly at first, broad farmland on either side under a pall of mist for the first five days. Perhaps the gods meant to warn us.

Redfist did not speak much, but he strode all day uncomplaining. His chin jutted, thoughtfully, and the beads in his beard clicked every so often as he moved. When we stopped at waystations, he did more than his share, as if in apology for the disruption to our plans. D'ri rode silently, and the ponies liked him a great deal. He had already begun preparing their hooves for ice, teaching them to be familiar with his touch.

There was no minstrel-strum at night, no child to chatter or sing Vulfentown drinking-songs, none of Janaire's soft merriness or Atyarik's companionship with another *s'tarei*. I had grown…accustomed to them, as I had to few others during my travels. Perhaps it was merely a measure of how long we had endured traveling together.

A companionable calm descended upon our trio. Redfist often hummed Skaialan melodies, his swinging strides marking the rhythm; on the second day I began to hum as well, a wandering counterpoint that sometimes slid through old childhood melodies. D'ri was content to listen, scanning the far horizon with a line between his coal-black eyebrows. Whether he expected trouble or was simply lost in his thoughts, I did not ask.

Instead, all our talk was of commonplaces—the

ponies, where to rest, the likelihood of the mist or the rain breaking in the afternoon, what piece of gear needed repairing or modification. The towns became villages with hostels instead of inns; the taverns became smaller and quieter. For days the blue smear of mountains on the horizon came no closer. It was late in the season for caravans to start, but we found evidence of their passing everywhere, especially in the waystations where the firewood was restocked and the straw full of still-green fislaine to keep the mice away.

The Road went only halfway through the Pass, they said. Even the Pensari did not encroach further upon the Highlands, and it cannot have been because of the ice alone. The giants are held to be fierce and unruly. I found Redfist tractable enough, though I could well imagine how an entire room of ale-loving, bearded mountains might cause concern to smaller folk.

Not to mention the smell, if they were as ripe as Ninefinger, or Redfist himself when I found him.

It was almost a moonturn before the mountains drew close enough to oppress and the Road began to rise more sharply. The house-roofs rose as well, peaks meant to slide rain and snow away like a courtesan's robe down his shoulders. The hinterland folk are closemouth, and drive hard bargains, but they are honorable enough. Especially when travelers mind their *own* mouths and manners.

We made good time with the ease of sellswords used to long journeys. At least we had not been in Antai long enough to soften. Sometimes we continued half the night, relying on Redfist's memory of the hamlets and their contents along the ribbon of Pensari stonework. Their Roads are not the broad curving avenues of the Hain or the flat-cobbled Shainakh streets; no, everywhere the Pensari ruled the crossroads are spokes of a wheel and the Road straight as could be, only barely altering its course a degree or two for some stubborn knot in the landscape.

Most of the time, they slice straight through such silly things as hills, or leap across torrents with their sturdy poured-stone bridges the Antai have lost the secret of making. There are stories of folk who may make stone live and grow as green things do, but I had never traveled far enough to see *that* witchery. In G'maihallan, such a thing could be done, but would perhaps be considered tasteless, and a waste of Power besides.

The frosts came, and soon enough the ground hardened. Carts on the road, heaped high with fodder or late produce, became fewer. The travelers we met were all streaming south, and no few of them must have laughed at the fools traveling in the opposite direction at that season. Then there were no carts and precious few travelers for a day or so, and the bite to the wind brought a rosiness to what little of Redfist's cheeks could be seen under red fur.

"Strange," I remarked at a nooning, as the ponies drank their fill from a clear, cold, fast-running streamlet already rimed at its edges. "There are no Skaialan traveling this road."

Redfist, scrubbing at his face and the back of his neck with a rag from my clothpurse, gave a short bark of amusement. "Noticed that, did you?"

I glanced at D'ri. His hair, neatly trimmed in the Anjalismir *s'tarei* style I remembered from my youth, was wind-mussed, and he looked as if he enjoyed the chill. At least it was not a heaving deck, and we had no disagreements to speak of. "Is it usually otherwise?" he asked.

"In this season? Those who can get through the Pass might not be able to return, but there's always a few." Redfist sounded grim. "Karnagh's probably closed tighter than a miser's wife, though. Corran gave a hint or two."

"Did he." *And when were you going to share the hints with me, barbarian?* I stroked the red-and-white pony's neck, enjoying the texture. Gloves and furs would soon be

175

necessary, and at least the *taih'adai* had taught me of the warming breath and a few other ways to keep ice from a G'mai. The nightly lighting of the fire without sparkstones had mixed results—either I could barely produce an anemic flame, or the pile of tinder evaporated into ash after a ball of flame devoured it wholesale. Still, I generally managed to call a fire into being without singing a roof or either of my companions, and that was well enough.

"Never thought it would come to this." A heavy sigh bowed his wide shoulders. "He was a cousin. Knew his father."

"He may not have known everything in the commission." I ran my fingers through thickening horse-fur, the vital haze of heat and life from the pony almost-visible. Every living thing cloaked itself in that trembling energy, Power begging to be tapped, released, shaped into harmony and brilliance. A continual wonder; how did other *adai* deal with the distraction? "But he did deliver it to the Guild."

"How much?" Redfist stared at the rag, working it around his callused fingers.

It had taken him a long time to ask.

"Two hundred pieces of pale Northern gold, each stamped with a wolfshead sigil." *A princely sum, indeed.*

"So. At least I am worth something." Redfist paused. "And new coinage. The mines…" A shake of his head, his red hair pulled back and tied in a club with a leather thong. "Tis a fool's errand, this. The Pass may well be closed."

"Do you wish to turn back?" I turned my gaze away, in case he could not admit it while watched. The trees had changed; instead of those who disrobed every autumn, those who drew their green finery higher against the cold surrounded us. They are secretive, those dark masses, and their pungency can fill the head just like mead.

"Aye." He wrung the rag with a quick, brutal twist. "Of course I do. But I cannot."

176

Fair enough. There are many things in life a sellsword would turn away from, if she could.

"What else will I do with my life?" he continued, shaking the poor piece of cloth viciously. "Sellsword until I am too old, then beg on a street?"

"I plan on opening an inn." It was out before I could stop myself. "Six rooms, waterclosets to match, hanging linens in the sun and foxing tax collectors."

The silence was deafening. Even the noise of a forest—creaking, birdsong, the vast echoing of the sky-roof itself—hushed.

Redfist threw his head back and laughed. It was not *quite* the reaction I had expected, but then, nobody expects to lay one of their cherished dreams before another. Not comfortably, at least. Who wishes to show their own foolishness?

"Lass," Redfist finally said, chuckles still burbling in his gut, "ye are the wisest sellsword I ever hae known. I thank my gods ye picked my pocket that night."

It was a kind thing to say. He may even have meant it. "Tis not much of a dream."

"I like it," D'ri said, smoothing the other pony's mane much as I had. "It seems an honest thing, and a gentle one."

"I am not sure of either." I stared at the horizon. "Tis more likely I shall end with three rooms and a single watercloset, or gut-pierced on a battlefield."

"Not while your *s'tarei* lives, Kaia." Soft, but with an edge, in G'mai.

I did not have a chance to reply, for Redfist folded the rag and tucked it in his belt to dry. "I shall nae stand to see *that* happen, lass. Come, we waste sunlight." As if *he* had not been the one to suggest a nooning.

That night, the first snow fell, and I began to dream.

I CHARGED. NOT STRAIGHT FOR *them, though that would have*

been satisfying, but to the left, where the shadows were deepest. Boots stamping, my legs complaining, ice underfoot and my left knee threatening to buckle again before silence descended upon me. It was not the killing snow-quiet I had discovered after my mother's death, but the white-hot clarity of battlerage. There is a moment, when the body has been pushed past endurance and your enemies are still all about you, when the last reserves inside a sellsword—those crockery jars full of burn-the-mouth, sweetheavy turit jam—are smashed. Muscle may pull from bone, bone may break, but the sellsword will not feel it for hours. The Shainakh call it nahrappan, the Hain a term that has to do with a cornered animal, and in G'mai it is called the s'tarei's last kiss, and it is said that even after an adai's death a s'tarei may perform one last action, laying waste to his opponents.

The Skaialan call it berserk, and there are tales of their warriors fighting naked except for crimson chalk-paint, touched by Kroth's heavy hand and driven mad.

Pain vanished. My dotani clove frozen air with a low sweet sound, blurring in a low arc as I turned sideways, skipping from cobble to cobble with no grace but a great deal of speed. The far-left Black Brother had an axe, and all thought left me as it moved, hefted as if it weighed less than a straw. Their soft, collective grasping burned away, I left the ground and flew, turning at the last moment, the arc halting and cutting down, sinking through fur and leather, snap-grinding on bone, and the Black Brother's mouth opened wet-loose as his arm separated, neatly cloven. The axe, its momentum inescapable, sheared to the side, and since his left hand was the brace for the haft it arced neatly into his next-door compatriot, sinking in with the heavy sound of well-seasoned wood.

Their child-high screams rose, but I was already past, and Mother Moon, I longed to turn back. The burning in my veins, the sweet-hot rage, demanded it.

Instead, I put my head down and bolted. Thump-thud, thump-thud, the street familiar now, each shadow turning bright-sharp as my pupils swelled, the taste in my mouth sour copper and katai candy. The Keep loomed ever closer, and if I could reach the end there was a narrow housefront with a door left deliberately unlocked. Once inside,

I could be up the stairs and out a high window, onto the roof-road again, up and down while the foul glove-net closed on empty air. There was an easy way into the Keep from there, if D'ri had reached it and secured the knotted rope...

A whistle-crunch. Another high childlike cry behind me as a heavy black-fletched arrow, its curve aimed high and sharp to give it added force as it fell, pierced a pursuer's skull, shattering it in a spray of bone and grey matter.

Kaia! *Thin and very far away, struggling to reach me through the rage.* Kaia, down!

"KAIA." A HAND AT MY shoulder, a short sharp shake. My hand flung out as if to ward off a blow—Darik caught my wrist, cold fingers strong but not biting. I had not reached for the knife under the almost-empty bag serving as my pillow, so I must have known it was him even in unconsciousness.

Redfist's snores echoed. D'ri must have been on watch. His grasp gentled, he touched my forehead with his other hand, as if he suspected a fever. "All is well," he said, softly. "You were dreaming."

"Was I?" The change from bright dream-daylight to the darkness inside a small waystation—the last on this side of the Pass, Redfist said—threatened to make me blind. I could not find enough air, and a touch of sweat along my nape immediately chilled me.

"It sounded very much like it." He crouched, easily, and as my nightvision returned I caught the gleam of his eyes.

I reclaimed my hand, rubbed at the solid sleep crusting my eyes. At least they were not frozen shut; thin threads of crimson on the banked fire were more suggestion than actual heat or light. "Again," I muttered into my palms. "The same thing, all the time." My Anjalismir accent had grown more pronounced of late, when I spoke to him. Sometimes it did not even cause a pang to hear his tender

179

inflection—or my own.

"Ah." He glanced at the waystation door, firmly shut and barred. The shuttered arrow-slits piercing the walls were covered with horse-blankets, to muffle the sting of night chill; the horses moved restlessly and the fragrance of their hides and breath—not to mention other, nastier odors—had vanished from conscious attention, we spent so long breathing them.

You do not allow the beasts to sleep outside this far north. The white winds can come without warning, and there are stories of livestock frozen stiff near the Pass when the blind storms descend.

"Will you tell me?" Uncertain, as if he expected me to take offense at the question.

No. Perhaps. "'Tis nothing. Merely dreams." I used the word for idle thoughts, things best put aside. Now I could see his expression, and a flash of something crossed his face. Was it pain? He nodded, sharply, and would have risen had I not caught at his sleeve. "D'ri..." The words trembled on my tongue. *They keep returning, and I think I saw Rikyat die, but...*

How many years had it been since I turned to anyone for...comfort? Was that what I wanted?

He waited. A hot, abrupt bite of shame pierced my chest. He was, after all, a very patient *s'tarei*, even among my kind.

"They bother me," I finally admitted, in a whisper. "I think...I think they may be *an'farahl'adai*."

He sank down, no longer crouching but sitting, The black silk and leather of a G'mai princeling was hidden under thick woolens, and if not for the tips of his ears or the severe Dragaemir beauty of his features, he might have been another sellsword, a comrade of convenience along the Road. "Not future-knowing, but otherwise." Reminding himself what it meant—the ways of Power are many and strange, and only a Yada'Adais can lay claim to knowing most their manifestations. Nobody knows all the ways but the Moon, as the proverb ran, the mistress of all hidden and secret places.

"I think...there was one, I think I saw how Rikyat died." My throat was dry, but leaving my sleeping-pad and nest of blankets to fetch a skin was a daunting proposition, even in night-boots. "And this one, you are in it, and the giant, Janaire and Atyarik too."

"At least they are safe in the city." But a vertical line appeared between his eyebrows. "If it is your Power breaking free, you may have visions. Like Janaire."

"I hope not." A shudder worked through me—before the battle with the Hamashaiiken, Janaire had *seen*. She did not speak much of it, but any G'mai child knows such a 'gift' is a burden and a weight upon the soul.

"It could be a temporary symptom." His palm against my cheek, warm though his fingers were cool. "I cannot guess, I am no Yada'Adais."

"Nor am I." *I have left my Teacher behind.*

His thumb feathered over my cheekbone. "Fear not, *adai'mi*. However the Power moves, we shall meet it."

Too fine for me by far, my *s'tarei*. The weight lifted from my shoulders, and I would have taken the rest of his watch, but he tucked me into my nest afresh and pressed his lips to my forehead, and I let him. If I dreamed again that night, I did not remember it.

THE PASS HAS A LOVELY NAME—*Armara-karnha*. The sound is pleasing and balanced, but the meaning is altogether different. Like any place that had ever heard of the Pensari, whiteness along the northern mountains is suspect at best and murderous at worst, and the name meant *the White Eater*. The crags are knifelike, massive teeth of some worldbreaking beast; wind constantly sliding along their

181

edges in a low moaning rising to a shriek as clouds from the south freeze and fall. There are pillars of ice in the higher reaches that have never melted, and stories tell of wind-spirits trapped in those long cloudy daggers, endlessly suffocating.

"Get down!" Darik barked, and I did not hesitate, throwing myself full-length into a snowbank. Something whistled near my hair, its buffeting blew stinging snow and freezing over me; I rolled, floundering in a sea of cold white wet.

None know why the harpies screech as they do, and their faces, gnarled into an expression of suffering, only add to the effect. The twin swellings on their feathered chests are full of venom, and their claws drip with it as they work, aching to drive into prey. They love meat, and will feast upon whatever they find, either freshly envenomed into quiescence, or frozen carrion. Their wings are broad, and powerful enough to knock a strong man down with their noisome breath. I have heard they can strip an brace of oxen in bare heartbeats, and I believe it very near the truth.

The thing shrieked as a fine-fletched arrow buried itself just under the juncture of its left wing. Bright hot blood spattered, already half-frozen by the time it hit the snow around me. I flicked a boot up, smacking its hindquarter to drive it aside as it fell, and its claws snapped a bare fingerwidth from my thigh.

"Kaia!" Redfist bellowed, and there was a glitter as the axe buried itself in the harpy's side just under the arrow. He almost clove the thing in half, and now I understood why he insisted one of us should always keep a watch overhead. It had come out of *nowhere*, and if not for my *s'tarei* I might have been reduced to mincemeat in a few moments.

Two more banked overhead, turning in great circles, their cries threadbare on the rising wind. Darik tore his arrow free of the corpse—the harpy was longer than I was, how could such a thing *fly*? He offered a hand, I took it gladly, and he dragged me up from the snow's wet clutching. The ponies rolled their eyes and cried out in fear, but fortunately did not bolt.

Perhaps they were intelligent enough to know there was no safety in fleeing down the Pass. Not in this weather.

Redfist did not seem to feel the cold. Perhaps it was his ruddy fur. D'ri and I both had the warming-breath now, but had Janaire not insisted upon training me, I might have frozen to death the night before we crested the Eater's throat and began sliding down on the other side. It was upon that high spine the harpy finally decided I looked like easy prey, being the smallest creature braving the ice.

Darik brushed snow from my fur-lined cloak, Redfist tore his axe free from the steaming corpse, its eyes now filmed and its feathers scattered. Seen this close, there was a certain beauty to its gray and white plumage, and I could see how the marks on its bony cheeks and proud, vicious beak only resembled human features.

I had never thought I would see a harpy in the flesh. Especially so close.

We half stumbled, half slid down the slope, but the two circling overhead did not dive until we were well away. They settled on the body of their former comrade, and the clacking, whistling sounds of pleasure they made were enough to feature in a nightmare.

"Tis a good thing our foster-son is safe," Darik muttered, as Redfist and I brushed the snow from his shoulders as well. My hood almost hid my face, and the tips of my ears were numb despite the warming-breath. "Those things could carry him aloft."

"No worse than wingwyrms." My heart pounded in my chest, and a thin trickle of icy liquid slid down my neck. "I would kill for a hot bath right now."

"Better than a bath to be had, lass." The corners of

Redfist's blue eyes crinkled merrily. His beard hung with ice, and every so often he would shake crackling bits of it free. "But not until Karnagh."

There was a rending of bone and a squabbling up the hill. I suppressed a flinch. "Thank you, D'ri."

He nodded, pressed his lips to my forehead quickly. Redfist watched with a great deal of amusement, and clucked at the ponies, soothing them.

That night, we sheltered in a small cave, burrowing like animals. In the middle of my watch—I took the first—there was a rumbling in the heights; it shook both Redfist and D'ri awake.

"Kroth guard us all." The barbarian's tone was hushed, and he pushed himself up on one elbow. "The mountains are hungry tonight."

I shut my eyes, imagining ice, snow, rock tumbling down the side of those sheer slopes, gathering speed and weight, crushing everything before them. "Avalanche," I said, quietly, in G'mai.

"I thought as much," D'ri answered. "Are they common?"

"He wants to know if they are common," I translated, pulling my cloak tighter.

"Worst in spring, when the melt comes." Redfist flopped back down with a groan. The ponies stirred restlessly, one hoof-stamping to express his unease. "But aye, common enough."

"Luck." I made the *avert* sign with my left hand. "Go back to sleep."

A fiveday later, we reached Karnagh.

ABOUT THE AUTHOR

LILI LIVES IN VANCOUVER, WASHINGTON, with two dogs, two cats, two children, and a metric ton of books holding her house together. However, referring to her as "Noah" will likely get you a lecture. You can visit her online at www.lilithsaintcrow.com.

ALSO BY LILITH SAINTCROW

The Dante Valentine Series

The Jill Kismet Series

The Bannon and Clare Series

The Strange Angels Series

Tales of Beauty and Madness

Romances of Arquitaine

Selene: A Saint City Novel

SquirrelTerror

Trailer Park Fae

Rose & Thunder

The Marked

...and many more.

CPSIA information can be obtained
at www.ICGtesting.com
Printed in the USA
LVOW12s1941010218
564917LV00001B/58/P